The Lost Letters of Sara Nelson

Clara Ann Simons

The Lost Letters of Sara Nelson

Clara Ann Simons

Index

Chapter 1

Samantha

I'm alone.

Again.

It's been half a year since I looked into the icy eyes of my ex-husband for the last time. Six months since I walked away from him, ending that chapter. Since the courthouse doors swung closed behind me, freeing me, yet leaving me feeling anchorless.

"You'd think I'd be reveling in this newfound freedom," I murmur to myself, taking a sip of my lukewarm coffee. No more tiptoeing around his changing moods. No more biting my tongue or playing the dutiful wife and mom. I get to be me.

But then, the million-dollar question: Who is 'me'? It feels like an eternity since I've known that.

The dimly lit café's worn-out mirror blurs my reflection. My features fade, edges becoming indistinct. "Guess it's a fitting metaphor for how I'm feeling," I whisper. Adrift, no direction, no beacon to guide me.

The fear lingers: will the fractured pieces of my heart ever meld with the strength they once had?

Frank. I chuckle bitterly. "He was supposed to be the one." At least, that's what I believed. But soon, our marriage felt like a repetitive tune and, eventually, a prison of our own making.

Do I regret it? Maybe. A bit. He gave me two beautiful daughters and memories I'll cherish. But the aftermath has left me floating, trying to rediscover Sam, the woman. Not Sam, someone's wife or mom.

"The first few days post-divorce were exhilarating," I confess, staring into the depths of my coffee. Like gulping fresh air after being submerged for too long.

But freedom has its price. Loneliness crept in. At first, it was a subtle shadow as the turmoil of divorce settled. Then, it became glaring. Friends? They vanished. Frank had been so skilled at pushing my true friends away.

I shake off those thoughts, forcing a smile. It doesn't reach my eyes. The café bustles around me: workers getting their caffeine fix, a student engrossed in his book.

And then there are the couples. Damn, they seem to be everywhere, taunting reminders of what I've lost. It's as if fate's having a good laugh at my expense.

I focus on one particular pair, my eyes misting over. Tucked away in a corner, their silver hair catches the morning light. They sit in silence, but decades of intimacy radiate from every nuanced gesture, every shared glance, every soft smile.

Watching the elderly couple a few tables away, there's a pang in my heart. Frank and I could never have had that. Not even if he'd danced the cha-cha in the rain to save our love. Growing old beside the keeper of your heart's every secret must be soul-deepening.

There's a stark contrast in the café, though. On the other side a jittery young couple probably on their first date. The girl twirls her spoon in her coffee, casting nervous glances. The boy compulsively rakes his fingers through his hair, stealing glances when he thinks she's looking elsewhere.

Their fumbling small talk makes me smile. When I catch those heart-struck eyes of hers, I want to march over and declare, "Honey, looks fade." I'd lean in and whisper that sure, he's a looker, but dig deeper. Find qualities that stand the test of time. Because if that's all there is, the flame will fizzle out. Too soon.

How I wish I could turn back time, hit the reset button. I'd look for something else. Something real. No doubt about that.

I take a deep breath, focusing on the dwindling steam from my coffee mug. As much as part of me yearns for that closeness again, I know I'm not there yet. I need to rediscover myself. Sometimes, solitude terrifies me, but it's a haven at other times. There's a unique peace in being alone, a solace in finding yourself.

The door swings open, and I am drawn to a familiar pair of eyes. Even from across the packed café, those entrancing green eyes feel like they're diving into the depths of my soul. It's been two decades, but I'd know them anywhere.

Olivia Mitchell. Besties since our diaper days. I've only followed her journeys on social media, with the occasional text. Always on the move, spreading awareness about societal issues, shaping the world with her documentaries one viewer at a time.

And here she is, like a gust of wind, blowing in out of nowhere.

Just like when we were kids, and she'd clamber into my room, scraped knees and that same infectious grin.

Her eyes still have that spark. The one that challenges you to seize every moment and live every day like it's a masterpiece waiting to be painted.

Before I can even process it all, she's wrapping me in a hug. Warm and lingering.

"Sam Thomson, as I live and breathe! Holy shit! How've you been?" She swings me side to side, almost as if she's about to shake the years off me.

Blushing, I manage a hesitant smile. That bashful side of me never really left.

When we finally part, her eyes have that old mischief. I take a moment to really look at her. The girl who used to drown in her oversized sweatshirts, tripping over her impulsiveness, has evolved into a force of nature, someone who'd make anyone take a double take. But her essence, that fiery spirit, remains the same.

I scramble for words, "What on earth are you doing here? I thought you were in Africa, doing one of your empowering women documentaries or something like that."

Olivia grins, "Something like that." She repeats. "Wrapped it up, just editing left. And where better to breathe than home? Did you know it's been over twenty years? My sister almost threw me out for staying away so long!"

Pausing, she waves over the waitress, ordering us a couple of coffees.

"Saw you through the window," she admits. "For a moment, wasn't sure it was you. It's been a lifetime, right? Then I noticed that tiny furrow between your brows when you're deep in thought. Some things don't change, Sam."

I chuckle, taken aback that she remembers such a minuscule detail, "You've changed, though. And damn, for the better. Whatever happened to the hoodie and ripped jeans girl?"

Throwing her head back, she laughs — a deep, uninhibited sound that feels like home. That laugh carries so many memories. Those never-ending summers lounging on the grass by the river, watching clouds morph while babbling about the randomest things. Laughing till our sides hurt, eating ice creams that dripped down our chins.

But high school turned tables. From being my constant, Olivia became the shoulder I cried on every time a boy broke my heart. Then Frank happened, distancing me from her and everyone who knew me as just Sam, not Frank's Sam.

"Can you believe it? Forty-two years old," Olivia exclaims, her eyebrows lifting in disbelief. "Beyond the glossy social media updates, tell me, what's life been like for you?" She intertwines her fingers with mine, reigniting an old, familiar warmth.

I find myself diving into the highlights, the personal snippets I never plaster over social media. My teenage daughters, the recent sting of divorce. Before I know it, the unmistakable prickling behind my eyes warns of tears, and I confess, "I'm feeling adrift, Liv."

Olivia leans in, her scent comforting, "You're brave, Sam, and you've made the right call. Prioritize you. Everything else, that direction you're searching for, will come when you stop chasing it so hard."

Desperate to steer the conversation away from my emotional precipice, I ask, "What about you? You've been pretty tied up, right? Globe-trotting with your documentaries?"

Olivia smirks, "Took me years to nail down what I wanted, but I've hit my stride now. It was about time I grew up," she jokes.

For reasons I can't articulate, talking to Olivia is a balm. A déjà vu of crying into her shoulder after high school heartbreaks, her hands running soothing circles on my back, or those gentle kisses on my forehead. She'd always anchored me.

"Thanks for the boost," I sigh, feeling the weight of it all. "It hasn't been a cakewalk, but I had to leave. Frank's overbearing nature was suffocating."

Olivia squeezes my hand, "Sometimes, to usher in something better, you've got to slam a door shut. As for loneliness, some are lonelier amidst a crowd, while others find peace in solitude. But hey, what do I know?" Her eyes, for a brief moment, betray a hesitancy.

"You're making a mark, making the world a better place."

She snorts, "Trying. With all the shit I've seen, sometimes faith in humanity's a challenge." Her eyes drop, shadows of sorrow forming.

Grinning, I give her hand a reassuring squeeze. She meets my gaze, a glimpse of that vulnerable girl hiding behind that confident facade shining through—only ever showing it to me.

Olivia's voice breaks the moment, "What's on your agenda today? I'd love to spend more time with you." She adds, her green eyes shimmering.

"I'm hitting the antique market. It's on the first Friday of every month on Main Square. A few books and trinkets are all my teacher's salary allows. You have no idea what keeping up with two teenage daughters costs, especially when Frank's contributions are...sparse."

"I'm in!" she suddenly exclaims.

"You? Into antiques?" My eyebrows shoot up in surprise.

"You'd be amazed at the treasures you find in those places," Olivia retorts with a playful shrug.

Our coffee cups sit empty, the remnants of froth drying on the rim. We step out of the café, and the biting New England winter air slaps our faces raw. I quickly zip up my jacket against the cold. As we walk, Olivia absentmindedly kicks a pebble along the path, retelling some tales from her travels.

I clutch my sides, laughing, as she recounts how a band of cheeky monkeys in Thailand made off with her hat, or the time she got ambushed by ants while taking a nature break behind a bush in Burkina Faso. "Ended up with a bunch of tiny bites on my butt! Hurt like hell for a week," she gasps between fits of laughter.

With each of her stories, I marvel at how unapologetically alive she is. My life with Frank and his oh-so-practical ways had dimmed my spirit, smothering any remaining spark. But here, with Olivia, that old thrill of adventure tingles in my veins, something I haven't felt since I was a teen.

Walking into my regular café earlier, I felt untethered, like my reflection was fading into the steam of my coffee cup. Even now, with labels like 'wife' and 'mother' weighing on me, I'm unsure who I am beneath them. But weirdly enough, just catching up with Olivia after all these years makes me feel more anchored, more alive.

Chapter 2

Olivia

When she laughs, genuinely laughs, I catch a fleeting glimpse of the Samantha I fell for decades ago. That bright-eyed teenager bursting with curiosity, always so radiant.

Yet, two hours in her company today, and I've coaxed out that laugh only thrice. I've tried, but three times in two hours isn't exactly a track record to be proud of.

It's as if her infectious joy has evaporated, and her spirit of adventure got locked away somewhere. The toxic relationship, that messy divorce, and the weight of single motherhood with two teens — they've taken their toll.

Despite it all, the magnetic pull she's always had on me remains unchanged. Not a day went by when I didn't wonder what life would've been had I voiced my feelings...

But her boyfriends—they came too quickly, way before I could muster the courage to share my emotions. Each of them, more insufferable than the last, slowly edging me out until I was left clinging to the fringes. I was relegated to the role of the friend who she barely spoke to but would cry on whenever another romance soured. If only she knew how each lament tore my heart apart.

Through my travels, I've come to believe in fate. Maybe time has chiseled away at her joy, but in this bustling antique fair, Sam is all I see. Her chestnut locks cascading over her shoulders, those tiny freckles dotting her nose that I used to find maddeningly cute. I think of the moles by her navel, the ones I dreamt of kissing a million times, and my stomach knots.

I shake my head, trying to dispel the thoughts. It's been twenty years since our paths last crossed. People change. Perhaps the current Sam is insufferably snobbish. But then, if she didn't harbor feelings for me back in high school, why would she now?

We weave through the fair's labyrinthine aisles, between cluttered stalls that brim with trinkets hailing from a bygone era. Every time she picks up an object, her eyes spark with that same childlike wonder I remember so vividly.

"You remember these?" she asks, breaking my reverie as she brandishes an old book.

"Your all-time favs. I recall how you'd get lost in those Nancy Drew mysteries," I respond.

Her fingers glide gently over the book's spine. As I watch her, waves of memories crash over me—memories of countless sleepless nights, whispering secrets in the hush of her bedroom.

"Back then, I truly believed I could do anything," she says, a touch of melancholy in her gaze.

"You still can," I shoot back immediately.

"You're too sweet, you know that?"

Sam tries to muster a smile but falls short. Her eyes glaze over with a deep-rooted sadness. Time, it seems, has robbed Samantha of her once indomitable spirit, reshaping her dreams, perhaps even shattering them. From where I stand, it feels like she's not living—she's merely existing, trapped in a monotonous cycle, a shadow of her former radiant self.

"Do you recall that school trip in freshman year?" I interject, showing her an old Niagara Falls postcard.

"You dared me to touch the water from a waterfall, and I slipped right in! I could've strangled you then," she recalls with mock exasperation, rolling her eyes. "Drenched head to toe, we almost missed the bus. I had to face so much flak for that misadventure. Good thing it was a smaller waterfall than Niagara," Sam jests.

"In my defense, it seemed like a fun idea then. I honestly didn't think you'd actually take a dive!" I counter with a grin.

"You've always known I was the clumsy one," she says, punctuating her words with a radiant grin, "Still am."

"We read this one together," I remark, picking up a timeworn book and flipping through its pages.

Sam scrunches her nose adorably, lost in the same memory as I.

My fingers dance over the rows of aging literature when a leather-bound tome draws me in. Upon opening it, the pages inside have been carved out, revealing a stash of old letters tied together with sun-bleached string.

"They used to make these as a sort of combination safe and hideaway," the bookseller interjects, noticing my interest.

Sam drifts over and delicately takes the letters into her hands. As she examines them, I try to etch every nuance of her face into memory: the furrow of her brow, the sunlight playing in her hair. I wish I could freeze this instant in time.

"They look so... romantic," she murmurs, biting her lower lip. "I'd love to know their story."

Without hesitation, I buy the book and the hidden letters inside. Judging by the grin plastered across the bookseller's face, the price might've been way too expensive, but some things are priceless. Sam's gaze is curious, yet she holds the letters close to her heart, guarding them as we exit the fair.

"These are from World War II," she breathes in wonder, "See this postmark? It's been passed by the censor. All's well."

"Censorship? Here in the States?"

She nods, "Makes sense. Had to ensure no soldier was leaking any secrets. Even the paper was unique—called V-mail or Victory Mail. Made for easy photography to save on weight and space during shipping. Once they arrived in the States, they'd print from the microfilm for the recipient."

"From a soldier?" I ask.

"No, a nurse. A certain Sara Nelson," Sam replies, her fingers tracing the faded ink. "She's writing to someone she simply calls 'M'. The words, Liv, they're...

breathtaking. I wish someone had ever loved me this fiercely."

My heart twinges at her confession.

She reads aloud, and every phrase is heavy with a raw yearning, a palpable longing. Sara Nelson was clearly, deeply in love.

"They're beautiful," I whisper.

"They are," Sam confirms, her voice thick with emotion.

"Do you think... Could we possibly trace her story? Find out if they ever made it, if they got their happy ending? Can you imagine returning these letters to their family?"

She smirks, "The lost letters of Sara Nelson? Sounds like the title of your next documentary."

"It'd be something," I muse, lost in the idea.

"I was joking, Liv," she says, her gaze suddenly sharp.

"I'm not," I quickly assert. "The story's there. Just tell me if we can trace these letters."

"You're serious?"

"Damn right."

Sam sighs, brushing a stray hair from her face. "Look, based on the stamps, we can find out which regiment she was with. The war's records are meticulous. Tracing her return to the States? Doable. Finding living descendants? Trickier, unless they've stayed put."

"And as a history teacher, doesn't this intrigue you? Pull you in?"

Sam hesitates, "World War II is my jam. But, remember, I teach teens about it. I don't chase ghosts."

My heart speeds up, "I want to try. But what I want even more is for you to be beside me while we do."

"Me?" She arches a brow in genuine surprise.

"Yeah, you. Where did that mystery-loving Sam go? The one who'd turn a game of Clue into a full-blown FBI investigation?"

She chuckles, the light dancing in her eyes. "She probably got sidetracked around sixteen or seventeen."

"We need to bring her back. Christmas break is just around the corner. We could chase down this story. Plus," I pause, taking a breath, "it means more time together. Thoughts?"

Truth be told, I gravitate more towards hard-hitting documentaries. This letter-chasing feels like it belongs in a Hallmark film. But the thought of spending more time with Sam? Irresistible.

She purses her lips, considering. "My girls are with their dad till New Year's Eve. I guess it could be... fun."

Before we realize it, our fingers fly over our phones, pulling up anything on Sara Nelson's regiment.

"They were stationed in Vermont before heading to Boston, then off to Europe in '44," she observes, her eyes narrowing in concentration. "These letters might've been her first from the frontlines. They were part of Operation Overlord."

I frown, puzzled. "Sounds more Middle Earth than history."

"Normandy Landing?" she offers.

"Ah, got it. From the old war movies my dad used to watch."

Sam nods, "Sara Nelson could've been there. Isn't it amazing?"

"We should head to Vermont then!" I blurt out, caught up in the excitement.

"Whoa, there. I meant research from the comfort of my couch. There's no way I'm traipsing off on a wild goose chase."

"But you said your girls are with their dad!" I argue.

Sam raises a hand, halting me. "There's this thing called the Internet? Super useful. You find something, we courier it."

"Where's your sense of adventure?" I tease.

Her laugh is soft, a musical note I've missed. "You've only gotten crazier since high school. Vermont in December? You have any idea how cold it gets?"

"But think of the snow-tipped mountains, the quaint villages..."

"You're nuts."

I grasp her hands, warmth seeping between us. "Don't you want to be a little nuts with me?"

Sam rolls her eyes, but the mischief lurking there, the echo of the girl I used to adore, makes my heart race. The prospect of a shared journey, hunting the final recipient of Sara Nelson's lost letters amidst Vermont's winter magic, feels tantalizingly close.

Chapter 3

Samantha

Another day. Another relentless dance with routine.

The shrill chime of the alarm at six-thirty pierces my dreams, pulling me into reality. The waft of freshly brewed coffee intertwines with the warm scent of buttered toast. I wake up the girls, their hair tousled, eyes half-closed, lunch boxes to be filled. A rushed peck on their cheeks, the shuffling of shoes, the monotonous drone of the car. The inevitable return to work. Dinnertime. A brief respite in sleep. And then, the carousel of life whirls again.

Days morph into months, months into years, and my life? Still painted in the same shades. Predictable. Stale. I'm not so much living as merely existing. It's a sad realization when the only desires left are projected onto your children. Like I'm channeling my thirst for joy solely through them.

That's probably why the mere thought of requesting a week off work ties my stomach in knots. But imagining a journey with Olivia? There's that familiar tug on my lips, an involuntary smile. She's always had that spark, that uncanny ability to infuse a piece of her relentless vitality into me.

Maybe it's worth the leap. An escape from the monotony of life.

Two weeks chasing down the ghosts of love letters written over half a century ago. No routines, no hastily gulped breakfasts, no lesson plans. It's reminiscent of that younger version of me, the one who believed in endless possibilities when Olivia Mitchell was by her side.

This entire escapade seems more fitting for an eighteen-year-old dreamer rather than a forty-two-year-old single mom. Yet, maybe it's time for some self-discovery. Oddly enough, the world seemed much clearer at eighteen, even if life didn't quite adhere to my scripted plans.

The knock on the door is soft, but it makes my heart race. I clutch the leave form to my chest, fingers damp, pulse erratic. Doubt creeps in, questioning the sanity of my decision.

Mr. Lewis looks up from his desk, peering over his vintage frames. His eyes, sharp yet gentle, study me.

"Samantha," he says, his smile amiable yet discerning. "What can I do for you?"

With an adrenaline rush, I lay out the golden opportunity before Mr. Lewis. "Olivia Mitchell is filming this documentary," I begin, "tracing back to the descendants of a nurse named Sara Nelson from the Second World War. It's going to be educational gold for our history class." I embellish every detail I can muster. The depth of the story, its historical significance, and although I suspect Olivia might be fibbing about the film, I leave that part out.

"Exams are done, Samantha. I don't see why you can't have the week off before Christmas," he interjects with a hint of amusement. "You hardly ever call in sick." Without further ado, his pen dances across the form, finalizing it with a stamp.

One hurdle down. Now, onto a more challenging one — getting my ex-husband to care for the girls. As a last resort, my sister is an option, but that would be taking advantage. I brace myself and dial his number.

"What now? I'm working," my ex-husband snaps.

Oh, how I want to unleash a tirade on him, but I swallow my irritation and pride. "It's a once-in-a-lifetime school project," I tell him, stretching the truth just a tad. "I really need you to be with the girls."

"I'm already taking them the first week of the holiday," he grumbles.

"They won't be any trouble," I reassure him. "You'll barely notice they're there." He pauses, then, "Isn't Olivia Mitchell that crazy girl from our high school?"

I roll my eyes, knowing he can't see me. "She attended our school, but 'crazy'? Not quite. She's a nationally acclaimed documentary filmmaker."

A tiny white lie. While Olivia is indeed recognized nationwide, it's within a niche market of documentaries. Ones that don't just entertain but ignite change. However, their audience remains, sadly, rather limited.

"Is she still... you know, gay?" he asks with a tone of feigned indifference.

I bristle at the insinuation. "I don't go around asking people about their sexuality, Frank. And it's none of my business. She's my friend. That's it."

In truth, I do know. Not because I asked but because Olivia's social media is typically awash with romantic photos. Lately, though, her Instagram feed has been partner-free.

He sighs, resigned. "Alright. But next time, plan better. Normal people don't just up and decide to shoot a documentary in Canada."

"It's Vermont," I correct, a smirk playing on my lips.

"Whatever. Canada, Vermont. Who cares? It's not something a rational person does," Frank snaps, and I can almost hear the disdain dripping from his tongue, the slick slide of his tongue clicking against the roof of his mouth.

His words grate on my nerves. To Frank, 'normal' people are the ones who have their lives scripted down to the last nanosecond. And then there's him, Mr. Perfect, the epitome of 'normal,' orchestrating not just his every move, but attempting to direct everyone else's symphony around him. How did I ever endure our marriage? And, more to the point, why did I ever say, "I do"?

Even after giving in, Frank's voice drones on in my ear, whining about reshuffling his oh-so-perfect routine. I take a deep breath, the tang of my earlier coffee lingering on my palate. Once, I would have bitten back, our voices clashing like thunder in a storm. He'd brandish his need for control, I'd raise my shields, and our conversation would devolve into a draining battle of wills.

Not today. I'm not letting him siphon off my spirit over something so trivial. "The girls will be at your place by 5," I state calmly, infusing my words with the politeness I'm not sure he deserves.

***

The afternoon blurs into a whirlwind of sleuthing. I delve deep into the records of the regiment mentioned in the letters, the crisp scent of old paper filling my nostrils. Sifting through the historical documentation of New England societies, especially those focused on WWII, the weight of the past seems tangible. Slowly, like assembling a jigsaw puzzle, fragments start coming together, offering hints about the enigmatic letter writer.

And there she is—Nurse Sara Nelson, not just a name on brittle paper, but a heartbeat from a bygone era. I stumble upon an aged photograph of her, taken before she boarded for Europe. God, she was stunning.

She was part of the medical brigade destined for a field hospital, shadowing the Third Infantry Division, who later played a pivotal role in liberating southern France.

A shiver courses through me as I sift through relics of the past, the ghostly imprints of fingertips on parchment. There's a magic in this, in illuminating the lives of the everyday heroes. It's exhilarating to see Sara Nelson come into sharper focus; resurrecting snippets of her life from fading ink and sun-bleached photographs.

Her tale beckons to be told. If only those envelopes had been preserved alongside the letters, deciphering this enigma would have been so much simpler.

Chapter 4

Olivia

The screech of contorted metal is a sharp drill in my ears. The truck swerves wildly, vaulting the median, hurtling straight toward our convertible.

Time seems to freeze just moments before the crash. My head whips towards Sam, catching the raw fear mirrored in her eyes. Before I can register anything else, the brute force of the collision tears into our car.

We tumble downhill, a nauseating descent that feels endless. All I want is to shield Sam from this nightmare. But when we come to a stop, tangled in a heap of twisted metal, one glance at her still form tells me our story might've been cruelly cut short.

"Shit!" I curse, jolted awake by the blaring of my alarm. "Fucking nightmares."

I open my heavy eyelids and swipe a sweaty palm across my forehead. I rarely remember dreams, but I could've done without this one. Thank god I don't buy into omens.

Twenty minutes past our agreed time, I pull up outside Sam's place, and there she stands on the porch, unmistakably impatient.

"What's with the luggage?" I raise an eyebrow at the sizeable suitcase beside her.

"And what's with the convertible in dead winter?" she shoots back.

"It's a classic, and it's all I've got. They don't make them like this anymore—a '92 Chevy Corvette C4," I brag, letting my fingers glide lovingly over its frame.

"Seriously? We're driving to Vermont in December, and you show up in a convertible?" Sam exclaims with disbelief, tinting her voice.

"Where's your sense of adventure?" I tease, my voice dripping with mock reproach. "It's winter-equipped, chains in the trunk and everything. What's not to love?"

"You're insane," she laughs, shaking her head as she throws her bag in the back. "Only you would think driving to Vermont in December in a convertible is a good idea."

Sam grins once in the passenger seat, fiddling with the heating vents. Stray strands of her hair catch the warm breeze, dancing with life as I rev the engine.

"I'd forgotten how much you hate the cold," I tease, a smirk playing on my lips.

"And I'd forgotten your winter uniform was a T-shirt. Talk about opposites," she quips, rolling her eyes with exaggerated drama.

"Ready for this escapade?" I ask, easing onto the freeway with heightened anticipation.

"You might think it's silly, but my heart's fluttering with excitement," she admits, letting out a dreamy sigh. "Feels almost... enchanted."

We coast in a comfortable hush, watching the world shift and morph outside. The snow, once sparse, thickens on either side, draping the bare trees in a pristine white blanket, infusing the atmosphere with a distinct holiday charm.

"You're still stuck in the '90s, huh?" Sam remarks suddenly, her fingers skimming my collection of CDs. "This music? Takes me back to our high school prom."

"That prom was a piece of shit," I blurt out, the memory stinging fresh.

"Sorry to dredge that up," she murmurs apologetically, "Hadn't really thought about it in years."

"Neither had I."

"Can you believe it's nearly 25 years since then? There's a reunion next year," Samantha says, a hint of nostalgia in her voice.

"They might celebrate. I won't be there," I vow.

"Of everyone we graduated with, you've probably achieved the most," she insists.

"Maybe because most of them were idiots. Except you," I add hurriedly, "In any case, I'm not going. High school was hell, and prom was the final straw. And your husband, at the forefront."

"Ex-husband. And nothing endearing about him," she interrupts.

"Whatever he is. The guy's always been a jerk. Never saw what you found in him."

"I didn't either. But for what it's worth," she pauses, placing her hand gently on my thigh, "I tried so many times to get him and his buddies off your back."

I fight the urge to sigh as warmth spreads from her fingers resting on my thigh, anchoring my attention to the road ahead. Still, the tingling in the pit of my stomach is hard to push aside.

"I didn't really care much about what your ex and his goon squad said," I admit, searching for nonchalance.

I don't mention how I had plans to ask her to dance that prom night. How I wanted to confess my feelings, assuring Sam she'd be happier with me than with Frank. But I was late because nerves sent my dad's pickup truck crashing into a tree. Five months of my work salary went into fixing that. And Frank and his pals "accidentally" spilling that ghastly red punch all over my dress didn't make for a great memory. Though punching him square in the nose? Kind of made up for it.

Soon, our memories drift back further—to days of late-night sleepovers under the guise of study sessions. I'd brush her hair, letting fantasies weave themselves into the strands. Picking up where we left off over two decades ago feels as seamless as breathing.

By early afternoon, we pass through a charming snow-draped town. Houses, painted in merry hues, mirror holiday postcards, and chimneys puff out comforting wisps of smoke.

"Can you imagine living here?" Sam wonders aloud, her eyes wide in awe. "It's beautiful."

"It's like we're inside one of those touristy snow globes," I jest, cracking the window just enough to let in a burst of frosty air.

With Google Maps as our guide, we soon pull up to the quaint inn Samantha had booked. My eyebrows shoot up in surprise.

"First stop on our journey!" Sam exclaims, her eyes widening with childlike wonder.

We grab our bags and tread on the snow towards the hotel's entrance. Inside, dark wooden beams crisscross a high ceiling, evoking images of a bygone era. A towering Christmas tree occupies a corner, and garlands in shades of white, green, and red hang by the windows, imparting a festive charm.

"It's like stepping back in time," Sam murmurs, turning slowly to soak in the details.

I lean in, whispering, "Back to the days of Nurse Sara Nelson."

A warm-faced lady, probably in her sixties, takes our details and leads us to our room. Antique wooden furniture fills the space, and an expansive window unveils a snow-laden garden. In the center stand twin beds, closely pushed together, and instantly, I'm aware of the tempting proximity that will place Sam to me at night.

"In the lounge, we have an assortment of pastries, hot tea, and apple cider throughout the day," the lady informs us. "Dinner is at 6:30. We do like keeping things a tad traditional here," she adds with a captivating smile.

"She reminds me of my grandmother," Sam jests.

I walk towards the wardrobe, the wooden floorboards groaning under my feet. "What do you say we do before dinner?"

"Feel like a walk, or would you rather cozy up by the fireplace and watch the world go by?" she asks, a playful glint in her eyes.

Oh, if it were just the two of us, the decision would be easy. Nothing would be more enticing than curling up with Sam on a couch, fingers brushing through her hair as the flames dance. But I suspect the lounge will be abuzz with guests. "A walk sounds lovely," I suggest.

Emerging from the shower, steam surrounds me as I pause before the fogged mirror. Damp strands cling to my face, my cheeks vibrant from the warmth. Briefly, I let myself imagine Sam behind me, her gentle touch tracing patterns on my back. Shaking the thought away, I grip the sink's edge, reminding myself that these fantasies only complicate our journey.

Bundled in snow boots and layers of wool, we brave the outside. The Vermont chill is a refreshing slap against my face.

"It's so... quiet out here," Sam marvels in a whisper, her wonder contagious.

"Yeah, it feels like time stands still," I murmur, brushing my fingers against her arm.

Her eyes brighten, and she links her arm with mine. As we navigate the frosted path, every little contact, even through our winter wear, stirs something deep within me. It's hard to believe that my feelings for her remain strong after all these years. Have I idealized her over time? Replayed our shared moments so often they've become more vivid than reality?

The path, adorned by snow-cloaked trees, ushers us to a hidden spot: a quaint stone bench facing a frozen lake, the world enveloped in a serene winter embrace.

"Can we sit for a while?" Sam suggests, brushing snow off the bench.

We settle side by side, our closeness palpable, and she gifts me a smile that sets my heart racing.

"It's incredible how early night falls here," Sam muses, gazing up at the twilight sky.

Above us, the unpolluted canvas unveils a breathtaking, star-dotted sky. We're both ensnared by its charm. The stars, like minute diamonds, sparkle against the vast, inky expanse. I'm barely aware of the soft weight of Sam's head resting on my shoulder until the gentle pressure of her warmth reminds me.

"We should head back," I murmur, wary of the words threatening to tumble out.

Sam raises her head, her expression a puzzle. There's a hint of a frown, questions lurking in her eyes, but she doesn't press. Silently, she stands, and we retrace our steps, the occasional brush of our arms igniting silent sparks.

By the time we return, guests are gathering in the dining area. We join the animated chatter, wine glasses in hand, until a chime from the small bell announces it's time to settle down. Across from us sits an older couple who, with their jovial mirth, might have just walked out of a Christmas card. They engage in spirited conversation with two middle-aged sisters vacationing to ski.

A server in crisp white and black pours steaming clam chowder into our bowls, a New England specialty. The roast that follows is equally mouthwatering, its savory aroma tantalizing my senses. We chat and laugh, the older couple proudly sharing pictures of their grandchildren.

But the atmosphere shifts the moment Sam mentions our quest: tracing lost WWII love letters. An unexpected hush blankets the table.

"What a delightful way to spend a romantic vacation," observes the woman across from us, her glance dripping with assumptions. Sam's face morphs into a shade that could rival a ripe tomato.

Her knee brushes against mine; she offers a fleeting, shy smile, and I swear my heart skips a beat or two.

"I think I might've had one too many," Samantha murmurs, nodding towards her empty wine glass as dessert plates are cleared.

Truth be told, the lengthy drive has me dragging, too, so we exchange pleasantries with our dinner companions before heading to our room.

Once inside, Samantha struggles with a stubborn necklace clasp. I move closer to assist. The brush of my fingers against the delicate skin of her neck, the small hairs standing at attention, sends a shiver through me.

"It was quite a day, wasn't it?" Sam says, turning to me, the edges of a genuine smile playing on her lips.

"It really was," I acknowledge with a sigh, lost in the moment.

Now, beneath the sheets in the dim room, I'm acutely aware of Sam's presence just inches away. The moonlight filtering through the window casts an ethereal glow on her skin.

I wrestle with my thoughts, but as I tune into the gentle rhythm of her breathing, my mind wanders. What would it feel like to pull her close? To feel the warmth of her naked skin, to trace soft kisses along her neck? To hear her sigh?

Chapter 5

Samantha

The silence of the night is deafening, echoing the hollowness I feel as I try to settle into the unfamiliar bed. Olivia's steady breathing feels both so near and yet miles away, a testament to the space between us, both literal and metaphorical.

I guess everything feels magnified in the darkness. Her presence, her sighs in slumber, the quiet rustling of sheets when Olivia moves. With each passing moment, a maelstrom of emotions churns inside me, threatening to spill over.

It's a deep yearning I feel, not just for a touch or intimacy, but for a connection. A connection that has been missing from my life for longer than I'd care to admit.

It's been six months since Frank and I went our separate ways. But even before that, our intimacy had been lacking. Now, it dawns on me. Our lovemaking had become mechanical, lacking depth. I'd often find more solace in my own thoughts than with him.

A tear slips down, silently painting the stark reality of my loneliness. This void has become an all-too-familiar companion.

Lying here, swallowed by the shadows, a profound sadness engulfs me. I mourn the years gone by, the moments and chances lost. It seems my identity had merged entirely into being Frank's wife and a mother.

Out of nowhere, these emotions blindside me. There's a whisper inside, suggesting the unthinkable. To close the distance with Olivia. To seek solace in her embrace.

But logic fights back. Olivia is my best friend. I had been married to a man for a decade and a half. I have responsibilities as a mother. And I've never seen another woman in that light.

A faint murmur from Olivia's direction pulls me from my reverie. Her face, bathed in the dim glow of the moon, looks so peaceful. If she knew of this inner turmoil, would she be understanding? Taken aback? Comforted?

Did I genuinely think of closing this distance?

I turn over, pressing into the pillow that holds the faintest hint of lavender, wishing for these whirlwind thoughts to settle. It's evident now; I've been starved of genuine affection and true connection.

As morning blooms, golden rays pierce the curtains, pulling me from a heavy slumber. For a beat, I keep my eyes shut, letting the warmth dance on my lids, and pretend I'm anywhere but this quaint Vermont inn— away from Olivia's bed, and the whirlwind of last night's thoughts.

Soon, the sound of running water and Olivia's cheerfully off-key rendition of an old Deep Purple hit has me smiling despite myself.

With a soft groan, I sit up, stretching, the weight of sleepiness pulling at my limbs. Olivia peeks from the bathroom, toothbrush in hand, her hair framing her face like a wild halo.

"Morning, sleepyhead," she chirps, eyes twinkling. "Hungry?"

I manage a half-smile, nodding before flopping back down. "Could you... maybe cover up a bit?" My voice comes out raspy, eyes darting away from her naked body.

Her brow arches, "What?"

"Clothes? Or at least a towel."

"Seriously? Sam, I've changed in front of you countless times," she protests, feigning shock.

"That was over two decades ago."

"So, I've aged that terribly, huh?" she teases.

I want to blurt out that it's the exact opposite. That last night, feelings stirred that shouldn't have. And now, her nakedness only muddles my thoughts further. But instead, I merely shake my head, forcing a smile, turning away to shield my reaction.

Breakfast finds us seated beside the elderly couple from the night before. They share they'll be here the entire week and have been doing some digging on our behalf.

"There's an old antique store on Main Street," the woman shares, her voice a hushed whisper as if sharing a secret. "Been in the same family for generations. Mornings, you'll find the owner there, an eighty-nine-year-old with a memory sharp as a tack. She might remember something about those soldiers who passed through town before heading to Europe."

Olivia and I exchange a surprised glance. We were nearly grasping at straws, but maybe, just maybe, this lead could shed some light on our quest.

"If only we were younger, we'd be right there beside you on your quest," the elderly man pipes up, his voice rich with the thrill of adventure, as if we were hunting down a lost shipwreck's treasure. "Such a romantic endeavor for a lovely couple like you."

A retort dances on my lips, ready to clarify we're not 'together,' but the genuine twinkle in his eye silences me.

Waving our goodbyes to the endearing pair, Olivia and I venture onto the quaint main street, searching for the antique store. It feels like a set straight from a Hallmark movie. Snow blankets everything in sight, making the buildings appear as ornate gingerbread houses, and the air sparkles with festive trimmings.

Nestled between a bank and an out-of-place insurance agency, the aged store beckons. Its window display is a nostalgic blend of timeworn books and period furniture. The door's bell jingles a welcome as we step inside, the rich scent of aged wood caressing our senses. Behind the counter, an elderly woman squints over chunky reading glasses, her scrutiny making me straighten.

"You two aren't locals," she observes, eyes darting up and down.

Before I can respond, a younger woman emerges from the back, motioning the older lady to sit. But Olivia, ever the forward one, jumps in.

"We're hoping to find some information about the soldiers who were here in '44 before shipping out to Europe. Specifically, a nurse named Sara Nelson? Someone thought you might recall?"

The old woman's eyes grow distant. "I remember those soldiers," she says, voice trembling with the weight of old memories. "Such vibrant times. The town's children, we'd tail them like lost puppies. They were here briefly, only two or three days. I was about ten. But Sara... Peston? I can't say I recall."

"It's Sara Nelson," I correct gently.

The old woman's hand drifts to her chin, stroking it in contemplation as if trying to summon a phantom memory. "Ah, yes, that. It's not ringing any bells. But the town was all aflutter with those soldiers. My older sister, she stole a kiss from one of them—though she'd deny it to her grave."

We allow her to weave her memories, absorbing the atmosphere of a town young and vibrant during the world war. I mentally envision her words as lecture notes.

As a history teacher, I know how invaluable her firsthand account would be to my students.

"You might want to check the local museum," the woman suggests, voice trailing off as if lost in thought. "They have quite a bit on World War II."

Finding the museum isn't hard. It's nestled inside an old brick structure, once part of the public library. The "extensive" exhibit on the war boils down to a single wall, adorned with faded photographs, maps, and snippets of wartime newspapers. Still, every piece tells a story.

Olivia and I study each photograph, taking in the young soldiers' hopeful smiles as they bid their loved ones goodbye at the train station. Townspeople gathered in masses, sharing tearful farewells.

My eyes catch a candid shot of soldiers outside a bar, jovial laughter frozen in time. And there, in the background, stands a solemn-faced nurse. My breath hitches as the caption identifies her: Sara Nelson.

"Look, Olivia! That's her! The woman from the letters!" My excitement bubbles over.

We rush to the museum's curator, who gives us a dubious look as if we've lost our collective minds. Unfortunately, the archives hold no further clues about

Sara. However, he points out that the soldiers' last known location was Rabell Falls, some thirty miles north.

He tries to guide us using a dated map, though we assure him Google Maps would do. Nevertheless, not wanting to hurt his feelings, we let him mark the spot.

As we head toward Rabell Falls, my mind races. Imagining Sara penning heartfelt words to her love, the guy perhaps wondering why twelve letters never reached him. And how overwhelming it would be for their relatives when we hand them these tangible memories.

The thrill is palpable.

Nestled in a warm corner of a cozy café before our journey to Rabell Falls, Olivia and I huddle over steaming cups of hot chocolate. Whiffs of cocoa entwine with the faint, buttery aroma of freshly baked cookies. Outside, snowflakes dance against the pane, casting a gentle glow around us.

"I don't get it," Olivia says suddenly, her eyebrows knitted in a quizzical expression.

I follow her gaze outside. "Rabell Falls?"

"No, this." She waves her hand, indicating our surroundings. "It's the end of December, practically

Arctic outside, and we're the only ones here. But right across, there's a Ben & Jerry's bustling with activity."

I laugh softly. "It's Vermont, Liv. Maybe they're just built to enjoy ice cream year-round. And isn't Ben & Jerry's a native treasure?"

She nods, sipping her drink. "Sure, bet ice cream in the world. But still, in this cold?"

From the whimsy of ice cream, our conversation drifts, swaying between memories and introspection. "You know," I begin hesitantly, "these past few years, I've felt lost, like I've been living someone else's life."

Olivia sighs, her tone gentler than before. "I think it started way before that."

"What do you mean?"

"I just remember back in high school," she says, her gaze distant, "you seemed to drift, trying to fit a mold."

I'm taken aback, a little stung. "It's not that easy, Liv. Everyone expected certain things."

Olivia reaches out, her fingers lightly touching mine. "I know, but it hurt seeing you not being true to yourself."

I lower my eyes, taking a moment to find the words. "Life happens. I made choices. Not all were right."

She tilts her head, her voice soft. "You had dreams, big ones. Remember them?"

I nod slowly. "I thought love was one of them."

"You never loved him," Olivia asserts with a resolute gaze, the air between us suddenly thickening.

"That's not something you can claim to know," I respond, trying to keep my voice steady, but the quiver betrays me.

Olivia studies me, her eyes softening but unwavering. "I see it, Sam. Deep down, so do you."

Each word is a palpable sting, nudging awake memories and feelings I've buried. The worst part? The gnawing realization that she might be right. I remember drifting away from Olivia in high school, and friends like her, as I cycled through short-lived relationships, each more draining than the last. It's like I was a magnet for heartache.

The warmth of threatening tears blurs my vision, and I look away, blinking rapidly to ward them off. The scent of hot chocolate fills my nostrils as I take a deep breath to steady myself.

"Hey," she whispers, reaching out. The cool touch of her fingers envelopes my trembling hand, grounding me. "I'm sorry. I came on too strong."

She rubs gentle circles onto the back of my hand, a soothing gesture. Her apologetic smile touches her eyes, and in that moment, it's her sincerity that pierces me, not her words.

"Sam," she murmurs, her voice a silken thread of encouragement, "you've always been fierce. A fighter. Don't let anyone, especially not someone like him, snuff out that fire."

Rising from her chair, she wraps me in a hug, tight and warm—a cocoon shielding me from my doubts. The weight on my chest lightens, and I breathe easier.

Stepping out into the crisp winter air, her fingers lace through mine, a tangible promise. We make our way to the hotel, the cold nipping at us until we're safely inside. Another hug, another soft peck on my cheek, and her whispered reassurances remind me why embarking on this journey was the best decision I've made in a long time.

Chapter 6

Olivia

The wheels of the car crunch over fresh snow as we veer off the main road, Rabell Falls coming into view. I crack the window slightly, letting in the biting Vermont winter chill and a rich scent of pine and firewood burning from distant hearths. It's intoxicating. Sam's eyes dance with a renewed sparkle, her breath fogging up in the icy air.

Driving through the heart of the town, every storefront gleams with holiday lights and festive trimmings. It's like the whole place was dipped in holiday spirit.

"If the last town was straight out of a greeting card, this... this feels like living within the card itself," Sam muses, her gaze darting everywhere, drinking in the festive ambiance.

"You haven't seen anything yet. The hotel? Even better," I promise, tucking a stray curl behind her ear—a move that brings a flustered smile to her face.

We trudge our luggage over the snow-powdered sidewalks, crossing paths with locals swaddled in scarves and woolen hats, their smiles wide as they offer season's greetings.

Pushing open the hotel's heavy oak doors, it's like stepping into a Christmas wonderland from a bygone era. Wood snaps and pops in a grand fireplace, spreading a welcoming warmth across the lobby, where clusters of guests engage in lively banter.

A sizable Christmas tree occupies a corner, its ornaments hand-crafted with names of regular patrons. Yet, our attention is undeniably drawn to a wall adorned with framed photographs of grinning soldiers.

And there she is again: Sara Nelson, her gaze deep and somber. A haunting beauty. It's clear, even in that snapshot taken before embarking for Europe, that her heart pined for the mysterious recipient of her letters, "M". The palpable affection in each word tells a tale of a love deep and true.

"These are from '44. This regiment helped liberate France in World War II," the hotel keeper chimes in, noticing our intrigue. "Stayed here for a couple of nights before heading to Boston to join the rest of the troops. We get their descendants visiting every year," he adds, a hint of pride in his voice.

Instinctively, I squeeze Sam's hand, a surge of hope coursing through me. We might just be on the brink of finding a living descendant of "M."

"Know anything about her?" Sam asks, her voice hesitant, pointing towards Sara Nelson's picture.

"Based on the uniform, she was likely one of the nurses who joined the regiment, bound for the field hospital," he notes, shrugging. "Beyond that, I'm not sure. We've got this storage in the basement—crammed with all kinds of old items, some from that era. Things left behind, never claimed. My grandpa, the history buff he was, cataloged them by date."

"People leave stuff behind often?" Samantha quips, eyebrows raised in mild disbelief.

"Oh, yeah, all the time. Back in my grandpa's day, even my father's, the items were more... intriguing. Lately? Mostly embarrassing sex toys and undergarments that folks are too shy to retrieve," he chuckles, a hint of mischief in his eyes. Noticing Sam's crimson cheeks, he hurries, "Didn't mean to make you blush."

We're handed our room key, eager for some rest and a refreshing shower. But as I push open the door, a surprise stops us in our tracks.

"Just one bed?" Sam's eyes widen.

"I swear I asked for two," I blurt, hands raised in a defensive gesture. "I'll go sort it out."

"It's fine. It's the holidays, and the place is packed. It's not our first shared bed rodeo," she teases.

"That was ages ago," I retort playfully.

She smirks, "No worries. It's a king-sized bed. I might not even notice you're there," nodding toward it.

As Sam showers, my fingers drift over the room's antique furnishings. How many travelers have stayed in this very room? What tales would these walls whisper if they could?

A soft knock interrupts my musings. The front desk man stands there, a woven basket in hand and a beaming smile. "Compliments of the house," he grins, handing over the basket brimming with homemade cookies and a bottle of sweet cider.

The immediate scent of cinnamon, sugar, and chocolate transports me back to childhood afternoons baking with my grandma. I can't resist a bite—the cookie melts in my mouth, leaving behind a trail of rich flavor.

"About the nurse you inquired about," he starts, "I've reached out to a buddy of mine who's big on World War II. He's coming over first thing tomorrow. Can't do it sooner, as we've got a Christmas dance tonight. All guests are invited," he adds with a grin.

He leaves just as Samantha emerges from the bathroom, draped only in a towel. I'm silently thankful for his timing; given her reserved nature, she would've been mortified. But if Sam keeps taking my breath away like this, I'm not sure I'll make it through this trip.

***

The hotel staff have outdone themselves with the holiday ball's decor. Each table glows with a radiant poinsettia, elegant candelabras, and silverware that whispers tales from a time gone by.

The whole room is draped in Christmas enchantment. Classic carols mix with the hits from the '60s and '70s, wafting from the speakers. The hum of spirited conversations, peppered with the occasional clink of glasses, fills the air.

Yet, my gaze keeps drifting to that mistletoe-adorned archway, imagining the feel of Sam's lips under it.

After my third gin and tonic, liquid courage nudges me. Setting down the glass, I stretch out my hand. "Dance with me?"

It's just a simple question, but my voice wavers, betraying my nerves. Sam grins and takes my sweaty palm, pulling a soft gasp from me. One I wish I could swallow back.

We start off a bit clumsy on the dance floor. Flashbacks of dancing with Samantha once—in her room, a practice run before her real dance with her then-boyfriend—cloud my mind. It crushed me back then, needing all my might to conceal the heartache and not to shed a tear.

But soon, the tension eases. Her hands find my shoulders, mine settle on her waist, and it's as if we've danced together a million times before.

"If you could have any Christmas gift, what would it be?" she suddenly murmurs, her curls teasing my cheek, making my pulse race.

"A time machine," I admit without hesitation.

She chuckles, "No second thoughts?"

"None at all."

"Where would you go? Hunting for Sara Nelson?" she jests, winking.

"I'd zip back twenty-five years, stand in front of a house, and hand a bouquet of roses to a girl I was madly in love with," I sigh.

She giggles, "So romantic! Would you want some superhero power to go with that time machine? Might as well wish big."

"Just the time machine. This time, I wouldn't let her slip away," I vow.

She teases, "That girl would've been one lucky lady. Do I know her?"

"Right now, I'm getting lost in her blue eyes," my voice quivers, heart hammering against my chest.

"Oh, Liv," she breathes.

"Roses are still your favorite, right? I hope I haven't botched it."

I try lightening the mood, but I can feel it—the electrifying current between us, both of us quaking from its intensity.

"I don't know what to say. You've never said anything to me before and..."

"I was a jerk," I interrupt, shrugging my shoulders. "And you were always busy dating assholes. I never found the right time... or the courage."

"Olivia, I'm speechless... I..."

"Don't say anything," I whisper, placing my index finger on her lips.

Heart pounding, I take her hand, and we stand under the mistletoe-covered archway. Sam looks up and lets out a long sigh, shaking her head slightly. She places her hands on my waist, rests her forehead on mine and we stand for a while just gazing into each other's eyes, our breathing ragged, until our lips meet in a wonderful kiss.

The last notes of the music fade away, and all I hear is the beating of my heart. The skin of her lips feels like the softest I've ever kissed. Sam sighs against my mouth as she feels the contact, her hands moving up, around my neck. It's just a caress, a light brush of our lips, but simply perfect. It conveys affection, desire, trust, tenderness. It is everything a kiss should be.

When we part, her face reflects a mixture of happiness and amazement.

"Wow," she whispers.

"Wow," I repeat like a fool, trying to catch my breath before my legs give out.

"That was..."

"Perfect," I interrupt.

"I was going to say unexpected, but I think perfect fits too," Sam acknowledges, biting her lower lip and raising her eyebrows as she lets out a long sigh.

I just shrug and curse myself for not finding the right words to continue.

"I guess a lot of things are starting to come together now," she says. "The way you looked at me sometimes like I was..." she interrupts herself, and a wonderful pinkish hue floods her cheeks.

"The most incredible woman in the world?"

"You're such a fool!"

All too soon, a couple stands next to us and indicates that they would like to have their picture taken under the mistletoe. The magic of the moment is broken, but my heart is still pounding so hard that I fear I might lose my balance at any moment.

"Do you want to go to the room?" I ask suddenly and immediately curse my lack of patience.

"Olivia, I... I'm feeling overwhelmed right now. It's too much to process. I don't even know what I'm feeling. I need..."

"Space, it's okay," I finish the sentence for her.

"Yeah, I guess that's the word I was looking for," she admits.

""Hey, Sam, it's okay," I reassure her, my voice soft and measured. "Nothing needs to happen here. This trip has been a rollercoaster for both of us. Whenever you're ready, we'll talk."

Samantha stands beside me, her posture tense, an unmistakable stiffness in her stance as we step out of the dimly lit lounge. My fingers brush against the smooth fabric of her dress, grazing her back, a gesture meant to soothe. But I can't tell; am I offering comfort or inadvertently causing more strain?

"It's not how you imagined this would go, huh?" Her voice breaks slightly, punctuated by a small shrug.

"Your friendship... it means everything to me," I respond earnestly. "If it makes you comfortable, I can crash on the couch."

She hesitates, taking a moment to find her words. "No, you don't have to. Listen, what happened was beautiful.

I'm just not sure I'm ready. Honestly, I'm in the dark about what I want right now. There's so much I need to reflect on, and tonight... well, it was unexpected. That kiss, the warmth and affection I felt, it's left me shaken. But I need time. Is that okay?"

I simply nod, feeling a whirlwind of emotions. We move to opposite ends of the bed, a gulf of space between us, our feet deliberately angled away as though even the slightest touch might tip the scales.

"Goodnight, sweet dreams," I whisper. The words linger in the air, caressed by the silvery moonlight seeping in through the window.

Chapter 7

Samantha

What on earth happened last night? The shock that we even kissed still lingers, not to mention the heartfelt words that spilled afterward.

Sleep eludes me, the weight of last night pressing hard. Sharing a bed with her, the woman I kissed, who poured out two decades worth of feelings that she's held since our high school days, is overwhelming.

To admit it to myself, that kiss was... just amazing. Any kiss from Frank, even during the height of our passion, doesn't hold a candle. It was tender, a touch of the divine, sultry. It whispered of promises, not just of love but of unwavering support. It told me that, given a chance, she'd stand by me, shield me, never let me down.

And that terrifies me.

I never looked at Olivia in 'that' way before. Yet last night, for a fleeting moment, I saw past the friend I knew. My mind raced, toying with the notion of us together. It was exhilarating, yet gut-wrenchingly daunting.

How would I explain to my teenage daughters that their mom's suddenly found a new facet of herself at forty-two?

Do I even... like women?

Perhaps it's not women. Maybe it's just Olivia. The person she is. Her uncanny ability to resonate with me, the way her presence calms my storms, the feeling of safety she blankets me with. There's an allure in her kindness, her effortless way of making me bear my soul, and damn, that smile of hers.

Maybe it's just that. Not about gender but about the soul. Or maybe not. Right now, my mind's a whirlwind, every thought a blur, slipping through my grasp. The sleepless night replayed countless scenarios, each more baffling than the last.

It's not like Olivia's story isn't clear. She knew she was gay in high school. Never did she bat an eyelid at a guy. Me? The polar opposite. Maybe society's norms blinded me, or I was too afraid to acknowledge it.

If there's one clarity amid this chaos, it's this — part of me wishes to erase last night. But how could I forget the softness of her lips, the tantalizing dance of her tongue, or the delicate moan I silenced with a deepened kiss?

Damn it.

Why this gnawing guilt? She's been my anchor since childhood. That one friend you can always lean on, no matter the miles between. Did we just obliterate that with one reckless moment?

I blink, letting my eyes adjust to the dawn filtering in. Olivia, cocooned in sleep, her hair splayed like a halo on the pillow. God, she's breathtaking.

Her steady breathing lulls, drawing an involuntary smile. For a split second, there's this urge—to brush against her, caress that cheek, tuck that stray strand behind her ear, meld my body against hers. Instead, I slide out of bed, ensuring I'm the very essence of stealth, unwilling to rouse her from her dreams.

A quick shower later, I tip-toe out of the room and head for the hotel's breakfast hub. It's buzzing, guests immersed in animated conversations. Grabbing a black coffee and a banana, I retreat to a secluded table, hoping to dodge any semblance of interaction. I need solitude. Time to think.

My phone lights up—a family group message. My heart leaps, reminding me how deeply I miss my girls, and it hasn't even been a week.

Emma: Hey, mom! How's the trip?

Angie: Fuck, Emma, you woke me up. Turn off the damn phone.

Me: Watch the language, Angie. Everything's great, Emma. How are you two?

My gaze is fixed on the three dots, thumbs hovering above the keyboard. How do I even begin to unpack this emotional labyrinth?

Me: We visited this quaint town called Rabell Falls yesterday. Looked straight out of a Christmas card. We should all come someday.

Angie: Is there a lot of snow?

Emma: Spot any cute guys?

Angie: I was still talking.

Me: Snow's everywhere. Picturesque. And Emma, I'm here assisting Olivia with a documentary, not hunting for love.

It's like those words just added an anvil to my chest. Memories flood in—sleepovers with hair braiding and shared dreams, lazy summer afternoons by the river, hours of talks. The way her emerald eyes started looking at me from the age of sixteen...

Damn, that look....

The longing was always there, simmering beyond friendship. I was just too naïve and terrified to notice it.

Emma: Dad thinks you're not over the divorce, says you're not ready for someone new.

Angie: He didn't exactly say that.

Emma: He did. Mom, Angie's trying to snatch my phone. Oh, by the way, met Dad's girlfriend yesterday. She's... really young.

I clench my jaw, my grip on the phone trembles. Just six months post-divorce, and he's still keen on orchestrating my life. Arrogant jerk.

Me: I'm glad Dad's moving on. When I'm ready, I'll know. He doesn't get to decide.

Emma: Gotta run, mom. Dad's girl made these crazy pancakes with whipped cream and chocolate. Heaven!

Me: Be good, okay? Love you both to the moon.

I set my phone screen down, take a calming sip of my now-lukewarm coffee, and my gaze inadvertently drifts to the entrance. Olivia strolls in, sleep still clinging to her. Our eyes meet, and she offers this delicate smile, a mix of mischief and warmth, as she approaches.

"Morning," she greets, her voice slightly raspy from sleep. "You're up early."

"Just didn't want to wake you. Thought I'd freshen up and grab some breakfast."

There's a palpable tension, a silence that wasn't there before on this trip. We sip our coffees, almost synchronized, steering clear of the elephant in the room. Dodging each other's gaze.

"We're glad you ladies chose our establishment," the hotel owner interjects, breaking the silence. "My buddy and I found some relics from '44, from the days the military stayed here. Some from the regiment before deployment, some from their return," he elaborates, placing a worn-out cardboard box on our table.

Drawn by an unspoken urge, we abandon breakfast and relocate to the cozy lounge. We settle on a plush couch, the grand fireplace looming ahead. The box is a silent sentinel between us.

We sift through faded photographs with lost sheens, rusty razor blades, assorted books. Every item is a story, every moment a memory waiting to be unearthed. The room is thick with the ghosts of the past and the uncertainty of our present.

"Look at this old flask," Olivia murmurs, her fingertips gently tracing the weathered metal. "It's probably seen hell and back. If only it could whisper its tales."

We sift through each relic with a near-reverence, letting the echoes of history wash over us. My fingers close around a small metallic object at the bottom, drawing out a vintage watch. Time had taken its toll on its gleaming surface.

Flipping it over, an engraving sends my heart into a startled skip.

"Sara R. Nelson. Time drags when you're not by my side. —M," I breathe out.

"Holy hell," Olivia whispers, her eyes wide open.

"Fuck. To lose it before heading to Europe?"

"Or maybe on the way back," Olivia counters, ever the optimist.

"Either way, it's gut-wrenching."

I let my fingers trace the engraving, a poignant token of their love story. The words stir a haunting nostalgia, tethering us to a time long past. "M" gifted Sara Nelson this, not knowing the old watch would never return to her side. Yet, their love remains immortalized in those simple lines.

Clutching the watch, its edges digging into my palm, tears blur my vision. My life's a whirlwind, and this simple inscription has left me raw.

"They sound deeply in love," I choke out, wiping away the tears that trail down my cheeks.

Olivia remains silent, her hand giving my knee a reassuring squeeze. It's her way, always anchoring me when the storms roll in.

The hotel owner chimes in, "About 45 miles east, there's a bigger town. They've got a Military museum, lots of stuff from WWII, one of a kind around here. Also, a historical society." He adds. "Maybe you'll find the answers you seek," he continues with a knowing smile. "About the watch, take it. If you find the woman's relatives or the letter's recipient, it's theirs. If not, you can drop it back here on your way home."

Gratitude laces our voices as we thank him. We head to our room to pack. As Olivia tackles her emails, I sprawl on the bed, catching a glimpse of my reflection in the mirror. The woman staring back seems like a mere shadow of her former self.

I've always tried to fit into a mold that was never quite right. Driftwood in life's currents. Have I really sacrificed my own joy, my own essence, for a life of mere monotony?

I merely exist, letting days flow past, armoring myself from more pain. Avoiding any risk. As hot tears stream down, I wonder, when did I stop being that fierce woman who believed she'd conquer the world one day?

Chapter 8

Olivia

The hum of my old Chevy Corvette comes to life, its engine's familiar purr a comforting backdrop as we pull away from Rabell Falls. Usually, that sound wraps around me like a warm blanket. Today, though, with the weight of everything unsaid between us, it feels different.

Beside me, Sam's lost in thought, her gaze aimlessly drifting past the window. I can't help but steal glances at her every so often. That soft crease marries her forehead, the absentminded way she nibbles her bottom lip—every little detail sends a rush of memories from just hours ago. The feel of that very lip pressed to mine, the surprised gasp she let out.

My fingers grip the steering wheel, betraying my anxious thoughts. I'm caught in the rush of new emotions, but I'm also treading cautiously. This newfound territory between us feels fragile, like the slightest misstep could shatter it. One misjudgment and the foundation of our long friendship could crumble.

My fingers drum an uneven rhythm on the wheel. That one impulsive kiss changed the dynamics between us. I can't help but wonder, did last night mean as much to her as it did to me? There's a palpable tension now, an intricate dance of newfound attraction mixed with the fear of the unknown.

The urge to pull over and just talk, to clear the fog of uncertainty, is strong. Yet, I understand she needs time, time to process, to figure things out. Patience has never been my strong suit, but for Sam? I'd learn.

She clutches Sara Nelson's old watch, almost as if she's seeking answers or comfort from its cool metal. The melancholic look in her eyes pulls at my heartstrings.

"Everything okay?" My words barely rise above the engine's purr.

"Yeah," she murmurs, her fingers still playing with the watch. "I just hope we can find Sara's relatives or maybe her lover's kin." The edge of her lips curve, a mix of hope and uncertainty.

There's a storm of thoughts behind Sam's eyes, but I hold back, knowing she'll unravel when she's ready. Gently squeezing her knee, I offer silent reassurance: whenever she wants to speak, I'm right here.

Suddenly, my attention veers to the roadside. Through the trees, the gleam of a frozen pond emerges, filled with the laughter and shouts of children. They're bundled in colorful hats and scarves, sweeping a puck back and forth using broomsticks.

"We need to stop," I declare, swerving the car before Sam can even react.

"You're such a child sometimes," she teases, the genuine smile lighting up her face, melting away the tension.

"I have a weak spot for ice skating," I confess, pulling up alongside the makeshift rink.

It's much bigger up close than it seemed from the road. A crowd, maybe fifty or sixty strong, glide across the ice, yet it's spacious enough for everyone.

As we near, a rental booth beckons, and soon, we're handed skates that fit us just right.

"Is it safe to skate here?" Sam inquires, a tinge of worry in her voice.

"We've done this every year, no casualties yet," the rental guy says, shrugging as if she'd asked if the sky was blue.

I catch Sam wrestling with her laces, her brow adorably furrowed in concentration. "Ready to hit the ice?" I call out, stepping onto the rink.

I ease in, gliding backward, while Sam grips a wooden railing, her footing unsure. She wobbles, her hesitation evident, but gradually, she finds her rhythm, skating with cautious yet determined strokes.

"Still got it, I see," I remark, skating up to her, our hands finding each other like they once did back in high school.

Quickly, we fall into a familiar rhythm, side by side, on a quieter patch of the rink. It's not long before she releases her grip, confidence gleaming in her eyes. She grins my way, triumphant. "I've got this," she declares, letting go.

Seizing the moment, I push forward, twirling swiftly, sending shards of ice flying.

"Show-off," she teases. That smile, the very one that's always had a way of softening my insides, is back.

Her laughter? It's always been my kryptonite. It transports me back to carefree afternoons spent together. For so long, Sam was my everything. She might've been oblivious, and I too timid to voice it, but she never quite left my thoughts. Maybe she's the reason none of my relationships ever truly stuck. How can they when you're haunted by someone else?

"Try keeping up!" I call out, skating ahead, a desperate bid to outrun memories and what-ifs.

Samantha hesitates for a mere moment, then with a playful determination, she's on my trail. Glancing back, I take in her flushed cheeks and strands of hair breaking free from her ponytail. Damn, she still takes my breath away.

I want this.

I want lazy weekends wrapped up with Sam beneath cozy blankets; the thrill of youth reignited with her by my side. The same unabashed laughter we once shared, now matured but still genuine.

I crave Sam. Deep down, I never really stopped.

This realization pierces me, seeping into my core. What if she's not ready? I know her well enough to see she's teetering on the edge of a decision.

Trying to shake off the weight of my thoughts, I approach her. She halts, her gaze distant, tinged with wistfulness.

"Everything okay?" I inquire, my hand gently finding her waist.

Sam jolts a bit at the sound of my voice, as though my proximity caught her off guard. A fleeting smile graces her lips.

"Sorry," she says with a slight shrug, "guess you're in better shape than I remembered."

I can sense it's not just exhaustion. Instead of pressing, I lead her to a wooden deck nestled along the lake's bend. "Come, let's take a breather," I suggest.

Lying back, I pat the space beside me, urging her to join. Our shoulders brush first, then our knees. I swear, the electric charge between us is palpable even through layers of winter gear.

Without a second thought, I loop an arm around her. Feeling her melt into me, Samantha exhales a weighty sigh. The world dwindles into the backdrop – kids playing, their inquisitive glances. All I perceive is the intoxicating scent of her hair. Everything else blurs out.

Enduring what feels like exquisite agony with her head nestled in the crook of my neck, Sam eventually sits up. "This was a good call, resting here," she remarks.

Watching the wisps of breath fogging up from her lips, I'm captivated. "Yeah," I agree, holding back the words bubbling up, revealing just how cherished those fleeting moments beside her were.

Samantha leans in, her body pressing into mine, her head turning. We're so close I can feel her warm breath feathering my skin, quickening my pulse. Sam closes her eyes, parting her lips slightly, and then... the harmony of a cappella Christmas carol shatters the moment.

"Good afternoon, ladies. Merry Christmas!"

"What the hell is that?" Sam's eyes fly open, her face a mix of shock and disappointment.

I mirror her reaction as we both take in the sight of a choir, all skating around us, decked out in period costumes, belting out carols.

"This can't be happening," I hiss under my breath.

Soon, a smile spreads across Sam's face, as if she's forgotten our almost-kiss, thwarted by the untimely interruption.

The carolers twirl and glide in time with the music. Their voices rise above the low hum of the small crowd that's gathered to listen, and I continue to curse their ill-timed appearance.

"This is absolutely magical," Sam whispers, her hand squeezing mine.

I elect not to respond, fearing I might say something I'd later regret.

As the final note rings out, the crowd claps enthusiastically, but the spark of a moment ago is extinguished. We remain together a while longer, the jubilant choir leaving the ice and the spectators dispersing.

"This is all just stunning," Sam exclaims, taking in our surroundings. "The snow-covered trees, the lake, it's like time stood still... it's a shame to leave," she sighs.

I can't help but agree. The setting is achingly romantic. If only those skaters had shown up a few minutes later.

It would have been so easy, so sweet, to close the small distance between us and kiss Sam's lips. To pick up where we left off last night. To finally banish all doubts and fears.

For a fleeting moment, I'm tempted to try again, but I only dare to gently kiss her cheek.

"I guess it's time to hit the road if we don't want to be caught out after dark," I murmur with a sigh.

Chapter 9

Samantha

Sometimes, the past has a peculiar way of seeping into the present, often when you least expect it.

As the rustic charm of the small town wraps itself around us, each brick, each cobblestone seems to whisper tales of yore. Here, amidst the snowy Vermont mountains, on a quest to find the recipient of misplaced letters, my own past tangles with the uncertainty of the present, a strange dance between fear and hope.

Main Street, blanketed in snow, is lined with shop windows glowing with cheerful colors, sparkling in the gathering dusk. Green or brown wreaths with enormous red bows hang from each door and lamppost, contributing to the picturesque sense of being in a Christmas card.

"Shit, it's like we've stepped into Santa's village," Olivia quips as she cautiously drives the car over the snow, following the directions we received from the previous hotel. "All that's missing are the elves," she adds.

Before I can respond, a blue sign catches my eye.

"There! Military Museum," I read aloud. "That must be the place the guy at the hotel told us about."

Olivia checks the GPS to confirm we've arrived at the correct address and parks in a vacant spot along the curb. The streets are virtually deserted, and as enchanting as the surroundings are, we're both eager to step into the museum to continue our search. There will be time for exploring the town tomorrow in the daylight.

The museum consists of only two rooms, but stepping inside is like stepping back in time. Sepia-toned photos of local soldiers cover the wooden walls. Glass display cases hold uniforms, medals, and other militaria, all carefully preserved.

The place may be small, even tiny, for a museum, but it's a treasure trove of local history. A tribute honoring the people of the area; young men who were whisked away to distant lands to fight in various wars.

We meander through the rooms, taking small, measured steps, absorbing as much as we can.

"It's just incredible," Olivia murmurs, halting before a display case housing photographs of local soldiers from the Vietnam War. "Most of them were barely more than kids. Hard to believe they went through such a hell."

I step beside her, my gaze falling on the somber portrait of a young soldier, no older than eighteen. Many of these boys left home for the first time to fight in a war they didn't comprehend, in a country they'd never heard of. Thinking of their parents, the fear they must have endured during battles, I must fight back tears.

We continue in silence, the muted ticking of an antique wall clock the only sound, pausing at every display case, soaking in each fragment of history.

At the back of the room, hunched over a cluttered desk, a man in his mid-sixties scribbles notes in a notebook. He looks up as we approach, peering at us curiously over his thick, horn-rimmed glasses. The museum likely doesn't receive many tourists, especially during this season.

"Welcome. I'm James, the museum curator," he introduces himself. "Looking for anything in particular?"

"We're interested in information about a local nurse who worked in a field hospital in France during World War II," Olivia quickly explains.

"Sara Nelson," he adds with a sigh of sadness.

"Do you have any information on her?" I ask, hopeful.

"A tragic story," he begins, nodding his head, his expression turning somber. "They say she was quite beloved in the area. A beautiful girl, always willing to help, with a melancholy gaze."

Suddenly, he falls silent and gestures for us to follow him. We trail behind him to a corner of the room, where a display case showcases a series of yellowed letters laid out on a black velvet backdrop. My heart skips several beats as I see the name Sara R. Nelson scrawled across three of them. Olivia gently rubs my back, sensing my quickened breath.

"Are these...?" I whisper in awe.

"They're letters penned in her own hand," the museum's curator confirms, nodding almost reverentially. "Addressed to her lover, someone only identified as 'M.' They're both tragic and romantic," he adds.

For some reason I can't quite articulate, the old clock and the letters before us have made Sara Nelson more real. She's not just a name; she was a flesh and blood woman who loved and suffered during the dark days of World War II.

Unable to physically touch the letters, we gain permission to photograph them with the display case open, trying to capture the frayed edges and the faded ink in as much detail as possible. The incongruity of photographing a slice of history with a sleek, modern cell phone strikes me.

I'm swamped by a wave of conflicting emotions. I yearn to know more about this woman. So much more. Yet, at the same time, I feel like we're trespassing on her secrets, infringing on her privacy. These letters reflect her passion, her desires, the very essence of this woman preserved in ink and paper.

They are carefully chosen words for 'M' where she chronicles the horrors of war, the fear, the death. Letters where she assures him that she loves him with all her heart, that she dreams every night of seeing him again, though she sometimes fears she won't survive the hell she's in.

"Do you happen to know the identity of the letters' recipient? The mysterious 'M' she mentions?" I ask hopefully.

The curator furrows his brow and strokes his jaw thoughtfully before answering.

"I've wondered that many times myself without finding an answer," he says. "The letters were donated many years ago, found in a dusty attic. There are various theories. There was a young man named Mark Levin from the next town over, Weston, which was Sara's hometown, but there's no proof it was him."

"So, you don't know if she ended up marrying 'M' after the war?" I press on.

"Oh, no, I'm certain about that detail," the man responds, scratching his head.

"Did they?" My heart feels like it's about to leap out of my chest as I wait for his response.

"Sadly, Sara Nelson died in a bombing in Southern France. She never returned to the United States."

"No... please," I whisper, my hand flying to my mouth as my eyes brim with unshed tears.

The news hits me like a freight train. I tremble, drowning in a sea of overwhelming, heart-wrenching sadness. It's as if the air has been sucked out of the room, and a heavy stone has been placed on my chest, making it near impossible to breathe.

I'd imagined a story of pure, unyielding love. Perfect love. The love letters, the pocket watch with the beautiful inscription. But reality has shattered that image into a thousand pieces, leaving only pain in its wake.

Gasping for breath, each inhalation a struggle, each exhalation a whisper of agony. I know it's absurd. This all happened nearly eighty years ago, and I never knew her, have no connection to her at all. Yet, her story, her tragic fate, resonates deep within my soul.

It's devastating. Her lost love, her unfulfilled dreams. A future stolen far too soon by a cruel war.

Tears blur my vision, and I blink rapidly in a futile effort to hold them back. But they roll unchecked down my cheeks, a mirror to the wreckage of broken hopes, of love promises that could never be fulfilled.

I feel a gentle touch on my arm, a comforting squeeze. Olivia.

Words fail me. I can't find them. How do you express a pain that isn't truly yours but feels as raw, as visceral as if it were personal?

The room's walls seem to close in on me, and I feel a desperate urge to escape, to find some quiet corner to process this whirlwind of emotions. A corner where I can cry.

All I can do is nod slowly, sobbing at the tragic end of a love story I had idealized, a story that promised so much and was cut short by the cruel hand of fate.

Suddenly, Sara's lover comes to mind. Did he ever read part of the letters? Was he aware of her fear of never seeing him again? How did he learn of her death? Was he able to move on?

There are still too many unanswered questions.

James, the museum curator, gazes at me with a blend of shock and sympathy. He mentions he'll ring up an old friend who works in the army archives, someone who can possibly trace any living descendants of Sara Nelson, but he forewarns it's likely an impossible venture.

Olivia wraps her arms around me as the man departs. I bury my face in the crook of her neck and weep, her tender strokes comforting against my back.

"It's so damned unfair, Liv!" I choke out between sobs, clutching her tighter. "Sara never made it home. She never reunited with the love of her life. They never got their dreamed-of future."

Each word is a dagger in my heart, a painful acknowledgment of a love that was brutally cut short, of dreams that remained mere dreams, their echoes haunting the hallowed halls of the museum. The intensity of it all threatens to consume me, and I hold onto Olivia as if she's my lifeline, her presence the only thing grounding me amidst the storm of emotions.

Chapter 10

Samantha

We remain seated in the car for a long while, encased in a silent stillness that hums with raw emotions. Tremors ripple through me, the weight of Sara Nelson's tragic end a relentless drill into my heart. I can't find a handle on the tumult of what I'm feeling.

"You know," Olivia whispers, her grip on the steering wheel white-knuckled, as if she's anchoring herself to the present, "one of my grandfathers was in World War II, towards the end. It could've been him, and I wouldn't even exist. Makes you think."

"It's horrendous," I confess. "You get used to thinking about those events as a distant past without really grasping how it changed the lives of countless families. It's... it's devastating, Liv. I don't even have the words to express my feelings right now."

Olivia lets me cry in silence, her soft caresses on my arm a silent promise that she's there, ready to listen when I'm ready to talk.

"How about we grab dinner?" she suggests after a while. "It's dark already, and I guess we won't solve anything by starving or freezing inside the car," she adds, a feeble attempt at lightening the mood.

I nod slowly, swiping the back of my hand across my tear-streaked cheeks as Olivia fires up the car engine and merges onto the road.

The snow has been coming down hard for the last half hour, and I'm thankful that Olivia is a good driver. Despite the winter tires, there are stretches where the old Corvette seems downright unruly.

The hotel is much smaller than the previous ones, but it still features a cozy common room with a crackling fireplace. The familiar scent of burning wood envelops us the moment we step inside, a comforting constant since we've arrived in Vermont.

Over dinner, between bites, I begin to open up about the insecurities that my marriage and subsequent divorce have left me with. The fear of not being loved, of not being enough for someone. I don't know why I'm spilling my guts like this. The scars from that time in my life make it hard to trust my feelings, but the heartbreaking revelations about Sara Nelson have left me raw.

"After years of losing my self-esteem, my identity as a woman, I'm terrified of being vulnerable again. I'm scared to open my heart, afraid of being hurt once more," I admit, averting my gaze.

Olivia reaches across the table, her palm upturned in an invitation. I lay my hand in hers, and she grins.

"Sam, you're extraordinary," she assures me, reassuringly squeezing my hand. "It wasn't your fault things didn't work out. I could've told you that long before you tied the knot with Frank. I'm surprised you lasted as long as you did with that man."

"I guess you get used to it and don't realize," I admit. "And then there are the girls. You delude yourself, keep telling yourself you're doing it for them, so they don't have to go through their parents' divorce. You try to convince yourself it's not that bad. The result is, at some point, you stop living. You just drift through life, the days all start to blur together, and before you know it, you've lost all ambition," I explain, my gaze shifting upwards.

"But it doesn't have to be like that. Not at all. You're stronger now; you've learned. You won't make the same mistakes," she points out.

"And I'll end up alone forever."

"Or you'll find someone who makes you incredibly happy," Olivia whispers, squeezing my hand again.

"And where am I supposed to find this someone?"

"How about right in front of you?"

"Do you really think that could work? We've been friends forever."

"All the more reason. We can skip a lot of steps, and your quirks won't scare me off," she jests.

"I don't have quirks, Miss Olivia Mitchell," I retort, shaking my head amusedly. "What about your documentaries? Will I have to accompany you to Africa or Southeast Asia for your shoots?"

"Lately, I'm realizing you don't have to go that far to fight injustices and inequality. They're everywhere. Plus, we're forty-two. I think we can handle a couple of weeks apart every now and then, can't we?"

"It sounds absolutely mad," I interject, rolling my eyes.

"Maybe. I can't guarantee it'll work. But what I can promise is, if you give me a chance, I'll spend every day trying to make you happy. I'll help you see yourself as special as I see you. Nothing's changed since high school. It's always been you, Sam. I wish I'd told you sooner."

"If I can't take the leap now, I certainly couldn't back then," I confess, letting out a heavy sigh. "This is all so confusing for me, Liv."

"I know. Take all the time you need. I imagine it's not easy. This is a new situation, but I think you're fighting your feelings. I don't exactly know what you're scared of."

"Everything," I admit.

Olivia smiles, and we order another bottle of wine, which we take to the common room. We settle on the couch in front of the fireplace, alone. The rest of the guests have already retreated to their rooms.

As we talk, her green eyes reflect the golden and amber hues of the flames, and it's nearly impossible for me not to get lost in them.

The scent of the burning wood saturates the room, flooding my mind with images of a bygone time, years filled with happiness, free from concerns. A time when life's complications hadn't taken root yet.

Every now and then, I feel the heat of her hand in mine, the touch of her fingertips tracing imaginary drawings on my thigh, creating a delicious tickle in the pit of my stomach.

"You know, Sara Nelson and M never had descendants," I point out after taking another sip of wine.

"I think I figured that out on my own," Olivia jests. "At least Sara didn't; M might have. Regardless, it'll be interesting if we manage to speak with some distant relative of that woman. Hopefully, the museum curator can dig up some more information."

"When you take it further and think about it, it's astounding that you and I are alive," I interrupt.

"How so?"

"Since prehistoric times, every person in our family line has had to live long enough to have offspring all the way to our generation. Isn't that incredible? Shit, if any of them had been eaten by a cave bear before they had children, that's it, you wouldn't exist."

"I think it's time for you to stop drinking for today," Olivia whispers, taking the wine glass from my hand.

"You know I'm right. We're talking about thousands of people, not one or two. And every single one of them was lucky enough not to die before having children. If you think about it, it's mind-blowing," I persist.

"Let's go to bed," Olivia suggests, tugging at my hand to get me up.

"Take a sip of wine, but don't swallow it," I order.

"What?"

"Just trust me."

Olivia shakes her head amusedly but does as I say. She takes a generous sip of red wine and holds it in her mouth. At that moment, I lean in towards her, wrap my arms around her neck, and kiss her lips.

"What are you doing?" She laughs, spilling some of the wine from her mouth onto our clothes.

"Fuck! You were supposed to pass me that wine... jerk," I mumble, elongating my words, suddenly aware that maybe I've tipped back one too many glasses.

"You're crazy," Olivia jests, a hand theatrically pressed to her forehead.

"Lucky for you, we're in a common room, or I'd undress you with my teeth."

"Come on, let's get to bed, Sam. As much as I'd enjoy that, I think you've had more than enough wine tonight. I don't want you to do anything you'll regret tomorrow," she whispers into my ear, offering an arm to help me stand.

My eyelids are heavy, my whole body feels like lead. I lean on my friend as we navigate to our room, wrapping my arms around her from behind as she reaches to open the door.

"The wine has nothing to do with it," I assure her, my teeth grazing her neck.

What happens next is a blur, but I'm certain it's far from romantic. I'm on my knees next to the toilet, Olivia holding my hair back as I purge dinner.

"Just like our high school party days, always there holding my hair," I joke, as she wipes my face with a towel.

And suddenly, it hits me. Olivia was always there, holding my hair or picking up my pieces. Lifting my spirits when I was down, supporting me. And all without asking for anything in return. Watching silently as I squandered my youth on fools who only wanted to have sex with me when she was the one who truly cared.

"I'm a terrible friend," I admit.

"Work with me here; it's impossible to get your pajamas on if you keep moving," Olivia reminds me.

I'm not sure how I make it to bed, but when I pry my eyes open, the first light of dawn is already sneaking in through the window.

Olivia is pressed against me, her arms encircling my waist, her face buried in the crook of my neck, her legs perfectly intertwined with mine in the most comforting spooning I've ever experienced. And now, devoid of alcohol's influence, everything I thought I knew about my sexuality starts to crumble.

Chapter 11

Olivia

I blink my eyes open slowly, the nape of Sam's neck filling my initial gaze. I'm nestled against her, my arm draped over her waist, hyperaware of the warmth radiating from her body. It takes everything in me to resist dusting that exposed skin with feather-light kisses.

My mind floods with the events of yesterday. The initial jitters of seeing Sara Nelson's newly revealed letters at the museum, the gut-wrenching blow upon learning she died in the war, never to reunite with her beloved "M."

Samantha took it particularly hard. Rarely have I seen her so shattered. I remember our talk, her fresh confession of discontentment with her present life, the way I laid my heart bare to her.

Damn it, for a moment, I thought things were going well. But her nerves had her guzzling wine faster than she could handle, destroying all possibilities. But we were so close...

Sam stirs in the bed, her brow furrowing slightly as she groggily opens her eyes. She turns to me and graces me with a sleepy smile.

"Hey," she murmurs.

"Hi yourself, sleep well?" I reply.

"Like a baby, but I think I need some ibuprofen; my head is about to explode," she admits, rubbing her temple.

"You did have a little too much to drink last night," I remind her.

She smiles again before slowly nodding in agreement.

"Can I ask you something?" she whispers, her voice barely audible.

"You know you can."

"Last night... I don't even know where to start... did anything happen? I mean, between us, did we... do anything?" she asks, fear tinging her voice.

"No, Sam, nothing happened, I promise. The furthest we went was when you tried to sip wine from my mouth, and we ended up staining our clothes. You'll see how hard it is to remove it; wine stains are stubborn," I reply, rolling my eyes dramatically.

"I remember that part," she assures me. "I also remember you holding my hair back while I was sick, but nothing after that."

"I helped you into your pajamas and got you into bed. You fell asleep instantly," I inform her. "But trust me, absolutely nothing happened. I'd never take advantage of anyone who drank too much, especially not you. I'd die if you regretted it the next day."

"Thanks, you must think I'm a mess."

"I've known that for a long time," I tease, winking at her. "Besides, isn't that what friends are for? Holding your hair back while you puke and helping you into your pajamas?"

We fall into a comfortable silence. Sam turns back around, and I wrap my arms around her again, parting her hair to plant a fleeting kiss on her nape. The way the tiny hairs there stand on end sends a shiver through me.

"What you told me last night... about how you'd spend every day trying to make me happy... it was beautiful," she admits.

"You remember that?"

"I was still pretty lucid at that point," she confesses, turning back towards me and leaning in for a kiss.

"Hold on, tiger," I stop her. "As much as I'm dying to kiss you, there are limits. You've been throwing up, and I suspect it won't be the most pleasant kiss."

"Not to mention your morning breath."

"I think yours is a lot worse right now," I joke.

"I guess I have to give you that," she admits, shrugging. "Can I take a shower first?"

"I can help with that if you want," I suggest, raising my eyebrows suggestively.

"I'd be too embarrassed to pee with you in there, and I need to shave my legs and... you know what else."

"Uh! Are we getting to that point?"

"You're going to miss out on what I was planning to do if you keep this up. It's already hard enough without you making it more difficult," Samantha protests, shaking her head playfully, her cheeks tinged a lovely shade of pink.

***

"Wow, you look beautiful, although with all the time you've been in the bathroom, you might as well be," I joke as I watch her come out wrapped in a white towel.

"I guess this is where you undress me?" Sam whispers coyly.

"I love it."

"Love it?"

"The way you blush. It always drove me crazy," I admit, moving closer to her and placing my hands on her waist to pull her to me.

"I'm very aroused but also very embarrassed," Sam confesses, squinting and shaking her head.

I smile and remain lost in her gaze for a long moment as I tuck a lock of hair behind her ear, caressing her cheek with the back of my hand.

I move a little closer, and the tip of her nose brushes mine before our lips meet in a wonderful kiss. Between muffled sighs, she bites my lower lip as I run down her back, letting the towel fall at our feet. I push her gently against the table, kissing her chin.

"How's it going so far?" I whisper into her ear as I run my thumb along the contours of her lips.

Samantha sighs. I slide my fingertips along her jaw until I reach her chin. She bites her lower lip and, eyes closed, tilts her head, offering her neck. I kiss her, run the tip of my tongue along her jugular vein until I reach her collarbone, slowly, drawing small moans from her mouth.

Our breathing deepens as my fingers move down her cleavage, grazing her tits. I circle her areola with my index finger, hardening wonderful nipples I'm dying to have in my mouth.

Pressing her palm on my chest, Sam pulls me apart. She raises her eyebrows, smiles, takes my chin between her fingers to kiss me, and now I'm the one muffling moans against her lips.

"Fuck, Sam," I sigh as we pull apart.

Her only response is a small nibble on my neck that gives me goosebumps as I rub my nose behind her earlobe, taking in the citrus scent of her perfume.

Sam unbuttons my pajamas slowly, making me shiver each time her fingers brush against my skin. I feel the caress of her boobs on mine, hearing soft moans as my right hand slips between her legs.

Aroused, Sam moves her hips, seeking more contact with my palm.

"Turn around," I whisper, placing my hands on her waist.

Samantha smiles and turns around. She spreads her legs, resting her forearms on the table. I slowly caress her buttocks, almost admiring them. She sighs.

I slide my fingers down her spine, watching every muscle in her back tense. I cover her shoulders with kisses, unable to stop myself from rubbing against her ass as we both moan in unison.

"Fuck me now, please," Sam begs, gripping the end of the table tightly until her knuckles turn white.

She cries out in pleasure, feeling two of my fingers inside her, spreads her legs apart, releasing her right hand to caress her tits. Sam moans, gasps, not caring that we are in a hotel. Continuous, long, muffled moans that drive me crazy with desire.

I slide my free hand down her pubis until I reach her clit. I rub it while continuing to make love to her, feeling her whole body tense, tremble, and finally drop to the table with a little cry. Relaxed, searching for breath.

"Fuck," Sam sighs, sitting up as she turns very slowly to place her forehead on mine.

She's sweating, her breathing quickening. Sam takes my hand and squeezes it, stroking it with her thumb before bringing it to her mouth to suck on my fingers and savor her arousal.

"I swear it was... intense. Very intense," Sam whispers, cuddling into me. "Why didn't I try this much sooner?" She jokes.

Samantha takes my hand and leads me to the bed, laying me face down on the mattress. Kneeling beside me, she slowly runs down my back, from my shoulders to my buttocks, making my whole body tremble.

She sits on top of me, leaning down to caress me with her tits. A soft, subtle touch that makes me shudder. I squeeze the pillow as she rubs her nipples on my ass, slowly moving down to the sensitive skin behind my knees.

Sam runs down my body very slowly, in slow motion, as if she intends to torture me. She caresses my calves, slides her palm down to my buttocks, slipping one of her fingers into my sex.

"I don't know how to go on," she suddenly whispers.

"Shit, Sam. You were doing it perfect, I swear," I protest desperately.

"I don't want to do it wrong," she insists.

"Anything you do is good enough for me. You can't go wrong right now. There's no chance," I assure her. "You have me literally dripping wet."

Her look has become sad. I can see the insecurity in her eyes.

"Let's try something. Get behind me," I propose, sitting on the bed with my legs spread.

Sam glues her body to mine, and I let myself fall on top of her, taking her hand and bringing it to my sex.

"Do like you would if you were touching yourself," I sigh, directing her fingers to my clit.

Sam rubs it. Somewhat fearfully at first, but soon, my moans let her know it's just what I need. I place my hand over hers, sighing each time she kisses my neck or moans excitedly next to my ear.

"Do you like it?" Sam asks between gasps.

"I'm going to cum," is the only answer I can give her.

"Cum for me," she answers back.

And hearing that line, knowing that dominant side of Sam that I've never seen before, turns me on so much that it hardly takes any effort to have a wonderfully intense orgasm.

"Suck my fingers," she commands, taking them into my mouth.

I suck them as if my very life depended on it, listening to her moans next to my ear as she bites my earlobe gently, until we both drop to the mattress, trying to catch our breath.

"You didn't mind what I did, did you?" Sam asks fearfully, drawing lazy circles over my nipples with her fingertips.

"About me cumming for you?"

"Yeah, that."

"You have no idea how much a sexually dominant woman turns me on," I reply, biting my lower lip.

Sam rolls her eyes and smiles, but our quiet moment is interrupted by the sound of an incoming call on her phone.

"Fuck!" she sighs, reluctantly getting up to grab her phone.

She walks naked across the room as she talks on the phone, my gaze glued to her ass like a fool, and suddenly her expression changes completely.

"Are you serious?" Sam's voice spikes, tension, and disbelief mingling in her tone.

A muffled response from the other end of the line reaches my ears, but the words themselves elude me. Sam's eyes are wide, her fingers tapping restlessly against the phone.

"Hold on, let me write this down," she hastily requests, her gaze darting around the room in search of a pen and paper.

Sam whirls around to face me as soon as the call ends, her eyes sparking with an intensity that sends a shiver down my spine.

"You're not going to believe this," she breathes, her words a husky whisper in the quiet room. "Fuck, Liv, you're really not going to believe this!" She punctuates her statement with a couple of triumphant jumps before collapsing onto the bed next to me, her excitement palpable.

"Are you going to spill, or do I have to guess?" I quip, my curiosity piqued.

"It was from the friend of the museum curator, the one who works in the military archives," she explains, her voice a low buzz of excitement. "He confirmed that Sara

Nelson died in a bombing during the liberation of France."

"Well, he could have saved himself a phone call," I interrupt, a bitter twist to my words.

"But Liv, he gave me an address!" she suddenly exclaims, her hands gripping my face as she leans in to plant a lingering, passionate kiss on my lips.

"An address?"

"Of a living relative!" She clarifies, her eyes sparkling with anticipation. "A certain Beth, the granddaughter of Sara's sister. She lives just about forty-five minutes away. Start packing," she orders, bounding off the bed and rummaging through her closet.

***

I guide the car carefully along the snow-laden side roads. Thick flakes have been falling relentlessly, piling on the windshield and obscuring our path, but our excitement over the new lead vastly overshadows any inconvenience.

"Can you imagine if Beth knows who this mysterious 'M' is? That would be incredible," Sam muses, her hands drumming on the dashboard like it's her personal drum set.

"That would be a game-changer," I admit.

"Do you think we should turn back? The weather's only getting worse."

"We'll be fine," I assure her, my grip tightening on the steering wheel. "I'm driving slowly, and this new lead is too important to wait. I won't let anything happen to us."

Sam grins, and her hand drifts to my thigh, dangerously close to areas that make it hard to concentrate on the road.

"If you want to die, you can keep doing that... but I'm not sure it's worth it," I tease.

"You're such an idiot," she murmurs, pulling her hand away.

A little over fifteen minutes later, we pull up to a farm on the outskirts of a quiet town. The main building, painted in a deep maroon, is blanketed in a thick layer of snow. A plume of smoke escapes from the chimney, adding to the quaint charm of the scene.

As we kill the engine, a woman in her mid-sixties appears at the door and beckons us inside.

"She probably thinks we're nosy freaks prying into her great aunt's love life. I hope she's not greeting us with a shotgun," I joke as we approach.

"So, you want to make a documentary about my great aunt?" she inquires, gesturing for us to take off our boots at the entrance before leading us to seats in front of a roaring fireplace. Two massive, indeterminate breed dogs eye us warily, ready to pounce at any sign of threat to their owner.

"That's right," Sam confirms. "We found some love letters your great aunt sent from France. We'd like to personally deliver them to her boyfriend's descendants and perhaps tell their poignant yet beautiful story. We want to respectfully portray the lives of ordinary people who endured that hell."

"To her boyfriend's descendants?" the woman asks with a smile, handing us steaming cups of what smells like herbal tea.

"Yeah, all the letters are addressed to a certain 'M.' They're beautiful letters, full of mixed feelings: love, fear, desire, longing. You wouldn't happen to know who her boyfriend might have been, would you? This 'M'?"

The woman's eyes twinkle, and she shakes her head in amusement. She studies us like we're a pair of city slickers with nothing better to do than chase after the boyfriend of a woman who died in 1944.

Finally, she rises, perhaps to tell a friend about the two nutcases who've shown up with some old letters from a great aunt she's never met. One of the dogs follows her while the other stays put, watching us.

About ten minutes later, she returns with a cookie tin and heads towards us.

"Do you think they're fresh? She took a while," I whisper to Sam, leaning in so the woman can't hear me.

Judging by the lethal glare Sam shoots me, my previous comment seems to have missed the mark. Wisely, I opt for silence as Beth retakes her seat beside us.

The woman opens the cookie tin with a kind of reverence, though it holds no cookies. Instead, it's filled with old documents.

"I never knew my great aunt Sara," Beth announces, her fingers slowly tracing her chin as if she's lost in thought. The firelight dances in her eyes, painting them with warmth. "But I highly doubt this 'M' belonged to a man," she adds, a mischievous twinkle in her gaze. "You see, I've always heard that Sara had a preference for women. She was rather famous around here for it. It was 1944, and being a lesbian wasn't exactly commonplace," she explains.

I'm certain my face is a perfect picture of shock, but Sam's expression is much worse. Her jaw is hanging open like a cartoon character, and she's struggling, and failing, to form words.

Beth eyes us with amusement, a grin tugging at the corners of her mouth. We must be the most entertaining thing she's encountered all day. Two out-of-towners rendered speechless by her revelation.

"You can keep this if you want," she suddenly offers, breaking the silence and extending the tin towards us.

"Are you sure?" I manage to ask, my voice barely above a whisper.

"As I said, I never knew my great aunt Sara. She was barely spoken of in my house; my grandmother preferred to keep her hidden. Maybe you'll find something helpful in here. All I ask is that if you ever make that documentary about my great aunt, you let me know. I'd like to see it," she adds, her gaze softening.

Sam quickly promises that she'll be the first to know, despite my own doubts that we can find the descendants of 'M,' who now appears to be a woman, or that we'll ever get to make a documentary.

"Holy cow! 'M' is for Mary," Sam breathes out, carefully inspecting a bundle of letters tied with a faded pink ribbon. "I'll always wait for you, Mary," she reads aloud, her voice choked with emotion and her eyes glistening with unshed tears.

Chapter 12

Samantha

Once more, snowflakes begin their dainty waltz as we park in front of the hotel. Night descends too swiftly in Vermont during winter, bringing with it a bone-chilling cold that seeps through, no matter how bundled up you are.

Olivia sighs, a soft, almost silent sound that's lost in the hum of the car engine. She's been eerily quiet throughout the drive. As she kills the engine, her fingers tighten around the steering wheel as though she's wrestling with her thoughts.

With the car's heat off, our breaths mist up the windows almost instantly.

"We should get inside before we turn into popsicles," she murmurs, her voice brittle against the silence.

I nod, too overwhelmed by the revelation about 'M' to voice my agreement. That seems to be the theme of this trip: confusion. Even I don't understand what's going on inside me, and the discovery that 'M' was a woman has only added to my bewilderment.

We shiver as we retrieve our luggage from the trunk, the cold biting at our exposed skin.

"Shit, even the North Pole must be warmer than this place," Olivia grumbles, her hands shaking despite her gloves.

The snow crunches under our feet as we trudge toward the hotel's entrance, and for a moment, I imagine being somewhere completely different. The moment we step through the threshold, a wave of heat washes over us, a welcoming contrast to the cold outside. I didn't wear my contacts today, and my glasses fog up instantly.

The reception area is dimly lit. Behind the counter, a young man, clearly bored, chews gum and raises an eyebrow at our arrival.

"Two beds, please," I request automatically.

Olivia glances at me, her mouth opening and closing a few times as if she wants to say something, but she remains silent.

"I'm sorry, but we only have two rooms left, and both have a single bed," the receptionist apologizes, still chewing his gum.

I exchange a quick look with Olivia. She smiles, the implication hanging in the air between us. One bed. An intimate space to share with her, something that both scares and excites me, because I still don't know if I want a repeat of what happened.

What does the future hold for us now? Can we just remain friends, or has that ship sailed? Am I ready for what comes next?

"We'll take it," Olivia cuts in, seeing my struggle to find words.

Once we're in our room, she opens the worn wooden door and flicks on the lights. It's cozy, nothing extravagant, but inviting. If it weren't for the queen-sized bed commanding the space, which sends my nerves into overdrive.

Noticing my apprehension, Olivia winks at me and turns up the heat while we strip off our coats and snow boots. Soon, the room warms up, banishing the remnants of the winter chill.

I sit on the edge of the bed, the old mattress creaking under my weight. I carefully pull the old letters from my bag and spread them out, handling them with a reverence that seems to fill the room.

"Hard to believe, isn't it?" Olivia murmurs, settling next to me. Her words hang in the air, a poignant echo of the thoughts swirling in my mind.

The few inches separating our bodies suddenly take on a new meaning. I run my index finger over the slanted handwriting, my heart pounding as I begin to read the first letter.

"They must've been so brave to love another woman in those times. It almost feels wrong to intrude on something this personal," I whisper, my voice barely above the rustle of the aged paper.

"I know," Olivia agrees, her brows furrowing in thought. "But because of us, their story can be shared with the world. It deserves to be told."

"So, you're certain about making that documentary now?"

"Let's just say their story has taken an unexpected turn," she concedes with a small smile.

"Do you think Mary had any descendants? Learning that her lover died in the war must've been shattering for her."

"It must've been ghastly," Olivia nods, her face grave. "If she has descendants, we'll find them."

The warmth from her body seeping into mine quickens my pulse. I take a deep breath, grappling with my own emotional turmoil. This morning, we let go. It was a moment of sublime bliss, something I haven't felt in years, but I didn't consider the complexities it would inevitably bring.

Now, the harsh reality is glaring back at me, and I can almost feel it smirking.

"Sam, what happens next is up to you," Olivia whispers, her fingers tracing a gentle path along my right arm, as if she can read the turmoil in my mind.

"Up to me? You think I can pretend it never happened?" I sigh heavily.

"No, that's not what I mean. We can't pretend it never happened, but whether it happens again, that's up to you. Whatever you decide, I'll respect," Olivia assures me, intertwining her fingers with mine.

"I don't know what I want, Liv," I confess, resting my head on her shoulder. "Everything's moving too fast, my thoughts are in a whirl. And finding out that 'M' was a woman..."

I avert my gaze, a futile attempt to hide the moisture welling in my eyes. Olivia says nothing, simply holds me tighter, planting a soft kiss on my temple.

Gradually, the panic recedes, replaced by a bone-deep exhaustion.

"I'll order a couple of sandwiches from room service. You lie down if you want," she suggests, gathering the letters and pulling back the bed covers.

Half an hour later, with some food in our bellies, our bodies fit together under the covers like pieces of a puzzle. With my head resting on her chest, her fingers threading through my hair, the future doesn't seem quite as intimidating.

"This is so much more comfortable than resting on a man's chest," I murmur, the words floating between us like a secret.

"There's no better pillow than a good pair of tits," Olivia teases, triggering a smile that fights its way through my fatigue.

In that bed, with our breaths rising and falling in harmony, the pull of sleep proves irresistible.

"Sweet dreams, beautiful," she whispers, her fingers tracing soothing patterns on my back. "Rest well."

***

I gradually wake, enveloped in the heat of the heavy blanket. For a moment, I forget where I am and snuggle back into Olivia's soft embrace. She's still deep in slumber, her beautiful features relaxed. Slowly, I extricate myself, careful not to disturb her rest. She murmurs something indistinct as I stir, but continues sleeping.

Retrieving another blanket from the closet, I wrap myself in it, a shield against the morning chill. Outside, the snow completely blankets the old Chevy Corvette, now an icy mound resting among other similar shapes.

My hands tremble as I untie the aged pink ribbon encasing the letters; its hue faded with time. I pull one out at random and start reading, seeking any clue to guide us closer to the truth.

Suddenly, as if by some Christmas miracle, the third letter reveals something amazing, almost erased by the passage of years.

"Mary Ellis

17 Willow Lane,

Weston, Vermont"

"I can't believe it," I murmur, reading the address over and over as if to etch it into my memory.

I power up my laptop, my heart racing. A quick search confirms that in Weston, right here in the same town where we are, a Mary Ellis lived on that very street until her death in 2001. My breath catches. She lived to be 92.

A few details about her emerge. She was a teacher, married, lived with her grandchildren following her husband's death, and was a beloved figure in the small community.

Tears well up in my eyes as I gaze at a photo of a white-haired elderly woman receiving an award from the mayor.

"It's her," I mutter in the quiet room. "It's Sara's Mary, her secret love." My eyes fill with tears as I observe hers twinkling back at me from the computer screen.

"Good morning, gorgeous," Olivia whispers, wrapping her arms around me from behind and kissing my cheek. "You're brilliant."

"We have to go there today, Liv. Can you believe it? They lived in the same town. We're so close," I exclaim, a jittery energy coursing through me.

"We should wait for the sun to rise a bit. It won't be easy removing that layer of snow from the car," Olivia points out, indicating the various mounds of snow outside.

"And to think those little snow hills were cars yesterday," I joke.

"For now, I can think of something we can do to kill time," Olivia sighs, nipping at my earlobe and sending chills down my spine.

"That spot is my weakness," I admit in a low voice.

"I know, that's why I do it," Olivia confesses, trailing her tongue along that spot while her thumb traces my lips.

"What would you like to do to kill time until sunrise? Play Parcheesi?" I jest, growing more excited.

"Can I ask for anything?"

"It's Christmas. Ask me whatever you want," I blurt out without thinking.

"Anything?" Olivia insists, raising her eyebrows.

"Well, don't get carried away," I warn, the undertone of excitement in my voice palpable.

A beautiful smile appears on her lips, and suddenly, she goes to the closet. Olivia rummages through her bag and returns, waving a pair of black leather handcuffs in the air.

"Do you want to tie me up?" I ask with surprise. "I've... never... never been tied up," I admit nervously.

"I want you to tie me, naked, to the headboard. And blindfold me," she adds. "You don't know how much it turns me on when I can't move or see what you're doing."

"And you let me do whatever I want to you while you're tied up?"

"Anything you want. No limits," she whispers.

"Fuck, you're starting to make me really nervous. Shouldn't we have a safe word or something?"

"That's for when I tie you up later," Olivia sighs before biting my earlobe again.

"Shit, Liv. You just took away any doubts I had," I admit, letting out a big gulp of air.

Tied to the headboard of the bed, completely naked and blindfolded, she looks beautiful. Olivia's in great shape, and her sun-browned skin from her recent trip to Africa reveals some bikini marks that highlight her beautiful boobs even more.

As I climb onto the bed, the mattress sinks, and her breathing becomes heavier. Her body tenses.

It's strange. I watch her and can't wait to make love to her. But there are so many options that I don't know where to start. Suddenly, I find myself with the power to do whatever I want. I decide.

It can be affectionate or rough, a slow torture, or quick passionate sex. The very idea of that power excites me to levels I never imagined. My sex burns with desire; it's almost painful, and I can't help but slide my fingers through it in an attempt to calm myself.

I gently stroke the inside of her elbow. I slide my fingertips across the delicate skin subtly, almost without contact, but enough to draw the first sighs from her lips.

"Don't pull on the cuffs, or you'll hurt yourself," I remind Olivia, leaning down to kiss her forehead.

I run my fingers up and down the inside of her arm, from wrist to armpit. Goose bumps rise on her skin, and, for a few moments, I hesitate to abandon foreplay and straddle her mouth.

I slide my fingers down her side. Her skin is soft, warm. As I run my fingers along the contours of her breasts, Olivia lets out a small moan.

I smile as I listen to her, drawing imaginary circles around her nipples without actually touching them. Now, the moans get louder.

I remember how much it turned her on when I took my fingers to her mouth last night, so I caress her lips. She tries to kiss me, but I pull my hand away. Olivia protests, though she smiles.

Instinctively, she spreads her legs wider, knees bent, soles of her feet touching. I reach between them, and her sex glows with arousal.

I caress the inside of her thighs. I want to go slowly, but I'm the one who can't take it anymore. I lick her sex slowly, as if it were ice cream or the most succulent delicacy. When she feels my tongue on her, Olivia lets out a small cry and tenses her abdomen.

"Please," she sighs.

I spread her lips with my thumbs, blowing on her clit. Liv tenses again, and I am unable to hold back.

I devour her sex. Literally. It's not a kiss; it's not a caress. I devour it as if my life depended on it. Olivia lifts her hips, writhes in pleasure, seeks to rub herself against my mouth. She moans incessantly. She gasps, pulling on the handcuffs and rising one last time to let herself fall onto the mattress.

"Fuck, that was amazing!" she squeals between gasps. "You're finishing me off, you're unbelievable."

I smile and remove the cuffs and blindfold. I lie down beside Olivia. She caresses my body, kissing me gently until I shudder.

And then, Liv makes love to me with painful tenderness. Every moan, every caress, transmits the words I still do not dare to utter.

Chapter 13

Olivia

Giant, languid snowflakes whirl across the windshield as I navigate a narrow road towards Willow Lane. It's the last known address of Mary Ellis, our enigmatic "M" to whom we've finally given a name.

Days of relentless searching have led us here. A journey of false starts, dead ends, disappointments, and joys. But at last, the story seems to be taking form.

In the passenger seat, Sam shifts restlessly, unable to still her excitement. The mere possibility of meeting someone who knew Mary Ellis, of gathering the missing pieces to our puzzle, electrifies her.

"I can feel it, Liv," she confesses, her voice quivering with anticipation. "We're on the brink of uncovering the truth."

Her infectious enthusiasm prompts a smile to my face. Of course, I want to find a living relative of this woman. I'd love to hear the complete story. Yet, just spending these countless hours with Sam, witnessing the evolution of our feelings, is reward enough for me.

My foot instinctively presses the gas pedal a bit too eagerly in an attempt to hasten our arrival. The car skids slightly, startling us both, yet stays on course. Flanking the road, snow-draped forests paint a picture of sublime beauty.

"I don't think I've told you yet," Samantha murmurs, "but I'm so glad you convinced me to take this trip."

"And I'm happy you rediscovered your adventurous spirit," I quip back.

"You can't imagine how much I miss those less complicated times, almost worry-free," she replies, her gaze tinged with nostalgia.

I slow down, freeing one hand from the steering wheel to intertwine our fingers. Sam strokes my knuckles with her thumb and falls into a contemplative silence.

"We can't change the past. What you can do is shape a different future," I reassure Samantha, squeezing her hand gently.

"Life deals you a hand. You have to play with the cards you're given."

"Documenting stories around the world has taught me one thing—life indeed deals you a hand, but it's up to you how you play it. Even with the worst possible hand, in places where they have nothing, some people never give up; they fight to move forward and change things."

"Like you?" she interrupts suddenly, lifting her gaze to meet mine. "You're one of the bravest people I know. Life has dealt you some hard blows, but you've always pulled through."

"I'm not easily knocked down. I can have my low moments, shed my fair share of tears, but I always find a way out. I tend to pick myself up and keep fighting," I assure her, nodding slowly in affirmation.

We veer right, bypassing the main entrance of the quaint village, the GPS guiding us through increasingly narrow streets until we reach our destination—a charming timber house, its exterior swathed in cheerful hues. The sight of smoke unfurling from its chimney, the scent of charred wood has become a familiar comfort since we arrived in Vermont.

"There it is!" Sam declares, her index finger pointing with certainty.

She bolts from the Corvette before I manage to engage the handbrake, stepping gingerly across the icy terrain.

"The moment of truth," she murmurs, her breath frosting in the chill as she raps on the door.

For what feels like an eternity, all we hear is the hollow cry of the wind around us. Our nerves simmer, taut as bowstrings. Sam's gaze meets mine. Her disappointment is palpable when suddenly—there it is. The soft patter of footsteps from within, twinned with the excited bark of a dog.

A sixty-something man swings open the door, peering at us with curiosity through thick, horn-rimmed glasses. Beside him, a scruffy mutt of indeterminable breed wags its tail eagerly, no doubt thrilled for the unexpected company.

"Can I help you ladies? Are you lost?" he inquires, taken aback.

"Did you know a woman named Mary Ellis? She used to live here years ago," Sam fires back, foregoing any formalities.

"She was my grandmother," the man discloses, and I watch as Sam trembles, electrified by the news.

Before anyone can utter another word, Samantha dives into our convoluted tale about the discovery of love letters, hidden away in a hollowed-out book. She details our quest for the elusive "M"—Mary Ellis. She weaves the story of all the breadcrumbs we'd followed to find her.

The man's eyes widen as he absorbs our narrative. I'm not sure if he's wondering whether we've been indulging in illicit substances or if he's merely dumbfounded.

"So, you found my grandmother's lost letters? The ones Sara Nelson wrote to her from the front?" he queries in a hushed whisper, his astonishment palpable.

"That's what I'm trying to explain," Sam affirms, her head bobbing in eager agreement.

The man alternates his gaze between us before a smile tugs at his lips, breathing life into his weathered features as if the past is reanimating before us.

"Please, come in. It's terribly cold out here," he suggests, realizing we're still lingering at the threshold.

Inside, the house exudes a warmth that belies its age. It's evident that generations have lived amongst the timeworn rugs, the faded cushions, and the framed photographs adorning the walls that span decades.

We huddle on a couch beside the fireplace while the man arranges a chair before us. He sinks into it slowly, almost ceremoniously, as if he holds the key to unlock the mysteries of a time long past.

"I was very close to my grandmother Mary," he begins, his voice a comforting murmur in the quiet room. "She brought me up, really, after my parents died when I was just a kid." The man's gaze turns distant, as if he's traversing back across the years, and his words hang in the air like an echo.

Suddenly, he apologizes and springs up from his chair, disappearing into the kitchen. The sounds of clinking china and the rich aroma of coffee fill the room. When he returns, a tray of steaming mugs and pastries in hand, his words pick up where he left off.

"It wasn't until my grandmother turned eighty that I learned the truth about her and Sara," he continues, his hands trembling slightly with the weight of the revelation. "Grandmother told me everything."

His face crumples slightly as he recounts the tale of Mary Ellis, her love lost to the war, and the stash of letters she couldn't bear to part with. His voice chokes with emotion as he describes how Sara's death in a bombing raid shattered her world.

"Sara Nelson was her one true love," he states, his gaze dropping to the worn floorboards. "My grandfather was a good man. She married him to move on with her life. I guess it wasn't easy to do anything else back then. But her real love was always Sara," the man repeats, his voice a low murmur.

We hand over the aged letters, and he treats them with an almost palpable reverence, his fingers tracing the worn edges lovingly before he speaks again.

"I don't think my grandfather ever knew," he adds, rubbing his stubbled chin thoughtfully.

Sam's hand finds mine, our fingers intertwining as she wipes away the tears that threaten to spill from her eyes. The story has left her raw, the emotions too fresh.

"My grandmother hid the letters in a book, one she'd hollowed out. She didn't want to throw them away, but she also didn't want my grandfather to find them," he explains. "It was the perfect hiding place. My grandfather was a humble man. He wouldn't touch any of those books."

"But if the letters were here, kept safe, how did they end up disappearing?" I interject, my brows knitting in confusion.

"After my grandmother passed, my sister took a few things. She needed money and sold some of the furniture and all the old books. Among them was the book that contained those letters. I searched for it, tried to get it back, but I never thought I'd see those lost letters again," he confesses, clutching the letters to his chest as if they were the most precious treasure.

"Have you ever thought about sharing Mary and Sara's story?" I ask, my heart pounding with the idea. "I'd love to make a documentary about them. I think their love story deserves to be remembered."

The man looks at me, startled, but then a look of genuine gratitude washes over his face.

"My grandmother would have loved that. She would have wanted people to know Sara Nelson, to know how much she loved her," he says, his voice barely a whisper, his eyes glistening with unshed tears.

"It's a beautiful story," Sam adds, her voice a mere breath.

***

"This visit has been ..." Sam trails off, her words lost in the cool, stale air of our hotel room.

"Quite intense," I finish for her.

"Yeah, I suppose quite intense," she echoes with a sigh. "Can you crank up the heat? I'm going to freeze to death in this place."

Sam shuffles closer to me, small steps that are hesitant but determined. We stand, face to face, our gazes locked. She wraps her arms around me, an anchor in the storm of emotions, and buries her face in the crook of my neck, her tears moistening the fabric of my shirt.

She lets the pent-up tension melt away, transforming into teardrops. I can almost hear the whirl of thoughts spinning through her mind. Not only is the story of Sara and Mary incredibly moving, with their forbidden love and tragic end, but Sam herself is wrestling with what she should do.

"Are you really going to film the documentary?" she whispers into my ear.

"I have no doubts, and I would like you to be with me, to help me. We could come back some weekends in January and February to shoot scenes and interviews. It would be a chance to spend more time together," I propose.

I gently stroke her back, peppering feather-light kisses on her neck. We sway together, our bodies moving in sync in a dance that might be slow but is brimming with tenderness.

"This story has given me a lot to think about," she blurts out suddenly.

"In what way?"

"I'm very confused, Liv. These days with you, I've been happy, really happy. Something that hasn't happened in a long time," she admits.

"Don't forget about the sex," I tease.

"I didn't forget about the sex. You've gifted me orgasms of an intensity that I couldn't think possible. More importantly, you've made me feel alive, I've begun to hope again. You can't even imagine what that means to me."

"Do you think you and I could build a life together?" I ask, pulling back slightly to look into her eyes.

Sam's expression turns thoughtful. She bites her lower lip as if her thoughts are waging a war.

"I care for you deeply, but there's so much to process. For me, all of this is a shock. Imagine discovering at forty-two that you're starting to fall in love with your best friend. Shit, Liv, I'd never even kissed a woman until literally four days ago."

"I can give you all the time you need. We can go slowly, at your pace," I assure her. "It's not like I'm moving into your place when we get back. Let's take it slow, okay? Filming the documentary will give us the chance to spend a lot of time together, and it's perfect for you to explore what you truly want."

"I'm very clear about that. What I really want is to be with you," she blurts out.

"Then what's the problem?"

"Well, I'm not someone independent like you, Liv. I have two teenage daughters, ties to our town, an ex-husband."

"We're not living in 1944 like Sara and Mary," I remind her.

"It's complicated."

"Good things often are. That's why they're worth fighting for," I assure her.

"I'm terrified. I'm afraid of making another mistake in life. I'm just looking for a partner who won't hurt me," she confesses.

"You know I would never do that to you. And, anyway, it's incredibly sad that you'd just settle for that. We're forty-two, for heaven's sake, we have an abundance of life ahead of us, so much to savor. You can't settle for someone who simply won't hurt you. You deserve a partner who makes you feel extraordinary, that sends shivers down your spine every time she undresses you, for whom every day spent together feels worth living," I declare, my words echoing in the cool, dim-lit room.

Sam clings to me as my words seep into the silence, her grip firm as if I were a lifeline in a tempest-tossed sea.

"I feel amazing with you," Sam confesses, her voice barely above a whisper. "It's just that...well, I've never in my life questioned who I really am or what I wanted to be. I've always played the role that was expected of me. You know that, I have done it ever since I was a child. In recent years, I've taken on the roles of mother, wife, teacher...but not as a woman. I don't know how to be myself."

"That's where I come in. I'll help you. I'll make each of your days unique."

"I suppose I should listen to my heart, shouldn't I?"

"If your heart's telling you to stay with me, absolutely," I quip, a playful wink punctuating my words.

Placing my hands on her waist, I pull Sam to me, and we kiss. She closes her eyes, her breathing quickening. Then, pushes my legs apart with her knee and, little by little, our kiss deepens. Sam explores the inside of my lower lip with the tip of her tongue as her hands slip under my pants to squeeze my buttocks.

Between gasps, I rock against her thigh, becoming more and more aroused as she rubs my sex, and one by one, our clothes fall to our feet until we are completely naked.

Dropping to my knees, I kiss her belly, making circles with the tip of my tongue around her navel. I lick the soft skin of her pubic area as Sam takes a few steps back and grips the bedroom table tightly until her knuckles turn white.

Samantha lets out a very long moan the instant I part her lips with my thumbs to kiss her sex. I run my tongue over it, slowly, very slowly, savoring every drop of her arousal, watching her shudder with pleasure.

Sam releases her right hand to root it in my hair. She tugs at it, drawing me into her sex the moment I lick her clit.

"Fuck!" she cries out, feeling my tongue on it.

I make small circles around it, alternating with the entrance to her sex. These last two days, I've learned that she doesn't like direct stimulation until she's already very aroused, so I circle her clit with my tongue, kissing it gently as Samantha trembles with pleasure.

She contracts her abdomen when I insert two fingers inside her. Sam moans, gasps, whispers words I can't make out. I search with my fingertips for that area that I know drives her crazy, pressing it again and again without stopping to kiss her clit until she clings tightly to my hair and, with a very long moan, rubs her sex against my mouth in small spasms of pleasure, suddenly becoming very still.

"Oh!" Sam sighs as I pull my fingers out before gently caressing her pubis.

"Did you like it?"

"Amazing," she whispers, squinting. "I swear."

I sit up and lead her by the hand to the bed. Sam lies on top of me, resting her head on my chest as she catches her breath.

And in this small hotel in Weston, Vermont, as I pull the sheet over her naked body and caress her back, I know I don't want to spend the rest of my life with any other woman but Samantha Thomson.

Chapter 14

Samantha

"You're quite the sweet tooth this morning," I tease, watching Olivia drown her pancakes in maple syrup as though the world's supply is about to run out.

"This is so good!" she replies, her eyes half-closed in ecstasy. "Authentic Vermont maple syrup. The best in the world," she adds, dipping her index finger into the sticky liquid before bringing it to her lips.

"I'm going to order toast with butter and jam; my blood sugar's going to spike just watching you eat," I say, shaking my head as I rise from my seat.

Soon, a sturdy, sixty-ish waitress approaches our table with the toast and a pot of freshly brewed coffee.

The hotel's tiny café feels like it's been plucked from a bygone era. The tables are laden with hideous red and white checkered tablecloths, and the Christmas decorations are overwhelmingly abundant. Garland hangs everywhere, and we've counted at least three Christmas trees adorned with twinkling multi-colored lights.

We'll rest here today before beginning our journey home. The snow has ceased, and Olivia wants to scout some locations for her documentary. I should be thrilled to return home. I'm eager to see the girls, but my budding situation with Olivia is making me nervous.

It's one thing to let go in the privacy of our hotel room. To enjoy her bare body, the exquisite orgasms she's gifted me over the past three days. To feel alive and unbound again. It's entirely another to return to routine and accept that I'm falling for my former best friend. Or explain it to my daughters or my ex-husband. Frank might have a heart attack.

"Are you okay? You're unusually quiet this morning," Olivia inquires.

"I guess I'm just tired. Someone kept me up quite late last night," I joke, raising my eyebrows in an attempt to divert the conversation.

"Perhaps we should start taking naps from now on," she suggests with a wink.

I smile and begin to slice into the toast, its golden crust giving way to soft insides, the butter melting down the sides. Suddenly, I gasp as I feel Olivia's bare foot sliding up the inside of my thighs beneath the table.

"What the hell are you doing?" I hiss.

"You need to relax more; spread your legs," she whispers.

"Absolutely not!".

"A little bit, please," Olivia begs, putting on a good girl face.

I look around, and the waitress seems very busy preparing breakfast for an older couple at the other end of the cafeteria, so I do as she asks and soon feel her foot caressing my sex.

"Fuck, Liv. I don't want us to get caught. We're not kids anymore," I moan, holding her foot, although I have to admit the feeling is wonderful.

"Are you turned on?"

"You know I am, but stop it."

"Finish your toast, and let's go to the bedroom," Olivia proposes, biting her lower lip.

"I can't believe this."

"You know what I need in the morning," she explains, shrugging her shoulders.

"Do you really need to have an orgasm in the morning?" I ask, surprised.

"Unless I'm in a big hurry, yes. I'm a morning woman," Olivia replies matter-of-factly. "It relaxes me."

"What if I'm the one in a hurry?"

"I have little fingers," she jokes, raising her hand and wiggling her fingers in front of me.

I roll my eyes and choose to concentrate on my toast, but I soon realize that Olivia is keeping an eye on me.

"You're undressing me with your eyes. Stop it, it's too obvious," I protest, lowering my voice.

"I'm fucking you with my eyes, to be more precise," she replies, making me really nervous.

It's peculiar. The way I feel around her. Never in my life have I ever contemplated anything remotely sexual with a woman. Not even in college when many of my friends took the opportunity to let loose and have a wild night or two. Back then, I was already with Frank, believing him to be the love of my life.

Now, though, every time I feel Olivia's gaze fixed on me, that primal desire in her eyes, it takes me to levels of arousal I haven't experienced since I was a teenager. And I don't know how to handle this sudden collision of fear and desire, because she makes me feel things no man has ever made me feel.

"Can I ask you something?" I pose the question, taking the last bite of my toast.

"Shoot," she replies.

"Don't you think we're moving too fast? I mean, Liv, this is all so new to me and..."

"Do you know what a lesbian brings to her second date?" Olivia interrupts.

"I'm clueless."

"A moving truck. Welcome to my world," she jokes, her grin stretching from ear to ear.

"Damn, you're such an idiot."

"I know, it's an old joke. I can't remember where I first heard it," she apologizes.

"I'm serious."

"We can take this as fast or as slow as you want. We have a few months together while we're filming the documentary. It's your call how fast we go. I'm not planning on moving in with you, well, unless you ask me to," she clarifies.

"How's everything here?" The waitress's voice startles me, interrupting our conversation.

"This maple syrup is just amazing," Olivia quickly responds.

"It's homemade," the waitress explains proudly. "If you'd like to take some home, there's a fair in town today with several vendors. I can give you the name of the person who sells it. There'll be live music, a little dance. You should stop by if you have time," she suggests.

We exchange a quick glance and nod almost simultaneously, certain that it would be a fitting end to a journey that's proving to be quite astonishing.

**

Bundled up against the chill, we step into the little fair, and it feels like stepping into the past. Likely, the whole town's here. I read on Wikipedia yesterday that Weston has a population of 566, and it seems like every one of them has come to this same spot.

Around us, Main Street is lined with booths selling everything from wool scarves to scented candles, carved wooden figurines, and the famous Vermont maple syrup.

A children's choir strains at carols while a crowd gathers around them. Parents and grandparents clap with pride or capture the scene on their cell phones.

"Do you want a hot chocolate?" Olivia asks.

I nod, adjusting my scarf. The snow may have ceased, but the cold is still biting.

As we wander hand in hand through the fair, Olivia shares various ideas she's thought of for the documentary we're filming about Sara and Mary. Our fingers interlacing feels so natural, as if I've been doing it with her all my life.

"Excuse me for a moment," I say, raising my hand and pulling my phone from my pocket. "It's a call from my daughters."

Olivia nods and smiles. She veers off to the maple syrup booth that the hotel waitress had recommended, while I step aside to a quieter area to talk without the music's noise.

My daughters' joyful voices ring through the phone, and soon, I'm grinning like a fool.

"I miss you both so much. We'll be heading back to-morrow," I inform them.

"Yesterday, Dad and his girlfriend took us to have pizza and then to the movies," my younger daughter blurts out. "They make a great couple."

"Shut up, you moron!" protests my older one, realizing her sister's comment might hurt me.

However, it doesn't. Not even a little. It's as if these days of discovering love with Olivia have helped me forget a large part of my past relationship.

"Mom, did you meet any handsome men?" my daughter Emma squeals through the phone.

At thirteen, she's becoming fascinated with relationships, which scares me a bit. I made so many mistakes because of that. I rushed into things. I started dating boys too soon. Many of them used me, feeling nothing for me but sexual attraction. I don't want that for my daughter, but her comment allows me to gauge her opinion.

"Well, I may have met someone..." I let the sentence trail off, my voice trembling, unsure of how to continue or if I even want to. Frozen.

"Mom, spill, please!" she yells, and I can practically see her hopping around her room, while her older sister rolls her eyes. "Who is he? Is he handsome? What's his name?"

"Who said it was a man?" I sigh.

Silence.

I press my lips together, instantly regretting my comment.

"Mom?" my eldest daughter asks cautiously.

"We'll talk about all this when I get home, okay?"

"Mom, were you with a woman?" she persists, her voice indicating more curiosity than criticism.

"Possibly. We'll discuss it later."

"Mom, fuck, this is... this is crazy," my eldest daughter blurts out, taken aback.

"Watch your language, Angie. Nothing's definite, I guess I'm still figuring out what I really feel and..."

"So, you're a lesbian now?" my younger daughter interrupts, lowering her voice to almost a whisper on the last word.

"There's no reason to whisper, Emma. There's nothing to be ashamed of. There are girls at your school who are lesbians, and others who are bisexual. Everyone is open about it, except for the usual idiots," I explain.

"But you're forty-two. I mean, you're not a high school girl; you're a teacher. How do I tell my friends that my mom has turned lesbian?" she insists.

"Sometimes you can be such a jerk, Emma," her older sister snaps back. "What matters is that mom is happy, that she finds someone who treats her well. What does it matter if it's a woman or a man?"

I fall silent, at a loss for words. Emma has always been a shy child. She takes refuge in books. Her opinions are heavily influenced by her father's ideas and are, to put it mildly, overly conservative.

"Just focus on being happy, Mom," Angie reassures me. "We support you with any decision you make," she assures me before hanging up the phone.

Once the call ends, I feel confused. I shouldn't have rushed into this. It's something that should be discussed face to face, in person, not over the phone. Angie took it well; one of her best friends is dating a girl, and they're perfectly fine. Yet, Emma's reaction worries me. Neither of them knows that the person I'm talking about is Olivia. That will complicate things even further, especially with Frank, who utterly hates her.

"Everything okay?" Olivia asks, closing the distance to hug me.

"Sort of."

"Something worrying you?" she presses.

"I'd rather not talk about it," I snap, abruptly ending the conversation.

I can see the disappointment in Olivia's eyes, but she doesn't push.

We distract ourselves for a while, wandering through the various stalls, avoiding the conversation I know I must have with her sooner or later. She glances absent-mindedly at an impromptu dance floor, but I'm not in the mood to join her.

"Want to go somewhere quieter?" she suggests, noticing my discomfort.

I nod and walk with her, hating myself for keeping her at arm's length on such an important matter. The silence between us grows heavier. Suffocating.

"Olivia, I..."

"What's wrong? Please, don't shut me out," she pleads, taking my hand in hers.

"This trip with you has been amazing. You make me feel things I never imagined possible," I admit, "but..."

"But?"

"Right now, I feel very insecure. I hinted it to my daughters, and Emma didn't react well. Liv, I don't know if I want to continue with this," I confess, lowering my eyes to avoid her gaze.

"Look at me, Sam, please," she requests, placing two of her fingers under my chin and turning my head. "It's normal to be scared. This is all very new for you. It's natural that you worry about what your daughters think, but they're two very smart girls. They'll want their mom to be happy, don't you think?"

"I don't know," I sigh. "I don't know anything anymore."

Olivia brushes a tear rolling down my cheek with her thumb, and the tenderness of that gesture makes my soul ache.

"When you're ready, I'll be ready," she whispers.

Overwhelmed, I crumble, shattering inside, and cling to her. I cry into her neck while she rubs my back, but nothing can soothe me at this moment.

"I want to go back to the hotel," I announce suddenly. "I'm sorry, truly. I'm sorry for ruining everything," I apologize, standing up and walking away briskly.

**

We don't speak. We just lay there side by side in the darkness. The scant inches between our bodies now feel like an insurmountable barrier.

I stare at the ceiling as if it might offer up an answer. Olivia tries to break the silence several times, to convince me that it will all be okay, but I can't bring myself to engage. I just want the quietude.

Her steady breaths tell me she's finally fallen asleep. It's nearly three in the morning, and we've both been awake, trying to remain still at opposite ends of the bed.

Tears escape me as I consider how different this night is. Yesterday, when we weren't in an embrace, Olivia's feet sought out mine in tender caresses. Tonight, the distance between us has never felt so vast.

Emotions jumble in my head: nostalgia and doubt, longing and panic. I turn my head and look at her silhouette, sleeping, peaceful. I want to hold her, to tell her I'm being an idiot. To promise her that I'll be brave and fight for our happiness. I wish I could assure her that I know she won't hurt me, that she'll take care of me, and I'll do the same for her.

But I don't dare. Emma's words have been too painful. Can I seek my own happiness without considering my daughters? Above all, I'm a mother and must put them before my own needs.

But as a woman? Am I willing to sacrifice my life again? My future?

Do I want to stop living and merely survive? Do I desire to settle into a routine I despise with all my being?

Can I accept a life without ambitions?

Without joy?

Chapter 15

Olivia

The silence between us grows deafening. I drive a bit too fast down the highway, gripping the steering wheel tightly as we leave behind the snow-dusted towns. The memories blur as we move forward. Those charming, Christmas-card villages where we once laughed together are now just remnants, echoes of the past I want to speed past on my way home. Joy has turned into pain.

Samantha spends most of the trip staring out the window, as if she'd miss something vitally important if she looked away.

"Do you remember that little bookstore in Rabell Falls? The one with the reading nook upstairs and a stack of old detective novels?" I ask, trying to strike up a conversation.

"Yeah," is all I get from Sam. She's indifferent, her gaze lost on some undefined point outside the car.

"Do you want to stop there on our way back?" I suggest.

She just shrugs, refusing to meet my eyes. My attempt to sound cheerful while asking comes off as pathetic.

"If you'd like, we could stop there for a bit. We have plenty of time," I press on.

"I miss the girls. I'd prefer we stop as little as possible," she responds tersely.

"Alright, but don't wet the car. If you need to use the restroom, let me know in advance," I joke, but my comment is met with complete indifference, not even a gesture from her.

I sigh and focus on the road. Snowflakes whirl on the windshield as we leave another town to our left. I can't even remember its beauty or its name anymore.

"Sam, I was thinking that..."

"Can you turn up the heat, please? It's cold," she interrupts without letting me finish my sentence.

I dislike driving at night, especially on snowy roads. As fewer cars pass, patches of ice form that could be dangerous if driven over, so I decide to stop at a roadside hotel we come across.

It's impersonal, utterly lacking in charm. A stark contrast to the cozy little hotels we stayed in on our way here. It's as if the hotel itself wants to mock the abrupt shift in our relationship.

"Shall we grab dinner? I spotted a restaurant a couple of blocks from here that looks promising," I announce.

Sam pulls a face I can't even identify and apologizes, claiming she's very tired and would rather stay in the room.

"Do you want me to order pizzas?"

"Do whatever you want," she replies without even looking at me.

I could have asked her if she wanted me to bring a couple of snowballs for dinner, and she would have given me the same answer. Any attempt at conversation today is futile.

"I'm going to check out the café across the street to see what they have, okay?" I suggest.

"Fine."

"Alright then," I say, a sigh lacing my voice as I push my chair back and leave the room. I need a breather, a moment's reprieve, or else I fear I might suffocate. My head's threatening to explode.

The diner I step into is humming with old carols, their cheerfulness lost on me. I'm adrift in my thoughts, the world around me blurring into insignificance. I feel like I'm sinking into an abyss.

A waitress, no older than seventeen and visibly bored due to the lack of patrons, hands me a bag filled with a couple of burgers and fries.

"Merry Christmas," she bids me farewell.

"Merry Christmas," I echo mechanically, my mind elsewhere.

Snow whirls in a violent dance outside as I trudge back to the hotel. The wind is a brutal, icy slap, rendering the air frigid enough to make polar bears shudder. The cold seeps into my bones, numbing my ears despite my woolen hat's feeble attempts at protection.

Our room's warmth is a welcome contrast, but Sam's demeanor is colder than the weather outside. She picks at her food unenthusiastically, pushing fries around her plate like a petulant child refusing to eat her vegetables. Her appetite is as absent as her cheer.

And then, that silence again. Draining. Crippling.

Desperation gnaws at me, and I bite my lower lip. When did our relationship veer so off course? Is she so terrified that she feels the need to push me away? If she'd only talked to me, not acted like a spoiled child, I could help her. Or at least, I'd try.

"Sam, can we talk about what's going on?" I whisper, walking on eggshells.

"I'm just tired," she insists.

"Please, don't shut me out like this. We can talk it through, whatever it is."

"I'm really tired. I'll talk to you tomorrow," she responds, her voice devoid of any enthusiasm.

Samantha heads to the bathroom to change into her pajamas. Just yesterday morning, we were intimate, and now she prefers to undress away from my gaze. This can't be a good sign. Am I misreading all this? Was it just a fling, and now that she's returning to her normal life, she wants to leave it behind?

I consider following her into the bathroom for a moment, but the walls she's erecting around her are insurmountable. Instead, I pull out my notebook and start jotting down ideas for the documentary. It's better to channel my frustration into something productive.

The tragic love story of Sara and Mary captivates me. Two women clinging to their forbidden love during

World War II. Their letters filled with passionate words, fear, and hope.

As Sam crawls into bed without a glance in my direction and starts typing on her phone, I envision their secret glances, their whispered affection in secluded corners, away from prying eyes. It pains me to know that their love never fully blossomed. Their story deserves to be told.

The night creeps on while hundreds of ideas whirl around in my head. Work distracts me from my sorrow. Still, I can't help but steal glances at Sam now and then. She sleeps at the edge of the bed, her body tense. Is there any trace left of the chemistry I thought we had? Or did I just imagine feelings that were never reciprocated?

Around three in the morning, exhaustion conquers me. I collapse on the far end of the bed. The night progresses, fraught with strange dreams. Nightmares where I can almost touch Sam's naked body, and then she pulls away.

I don't mind giving her all the space she needs. I'm okay with keeping pace with her. But I do want to have a conversation about it. I wish to know what's going on in her mind. Why she's building barriers between us.

Chapter 16

Samantha

The ride back from Vermont is a silence that swallows sound whole. It's a weight on my chest, like someone's placed a granite slab on me. I try to distract myself, staring out the window, but even the charming snow-draped villages can't soothe my turmoil. What seemed magical days ago, now barely registers.

Two days back, driving from Rabell Falls to Weston, my mind was a free bird, sketching out a summer trip with Olivia. Imagining our old Corvette, top down, her hair a wild dance in the wind. Today, it's as if someone's hit a switch, plunging my future into darkness.

Olivia tries to strike up conversation now and then, but her attempts are half-hearted, not even expecting a reply. Guilt gnaws at me for giving her nothing but monosyllabic answers, grunts, or just plain silence.

The winding Vermont roads seem to stretch into forever, and my daughter Emma's words weigh on me like a ton of bricks.

As we near home, the crisp, icy air, the scent of pine, fades. It's replaced by exhaust fumes, the salty twilight air, dirty snow piles stacked up along the street edges.

The quaint backstreets, with their family shops decked out for Christmas, morph into personality-less suburbs, their houses all identical and flanked by massive malls.

When we finally pull up to my house, the tension between us is so thick it nearly chokes me. Olivia's piercing green eyes watch as I lug our suitcases out, but she maintains a safe distance, not a trace of the soft caresses we shared days ago.

"Thanks for everything. We'll keep in touch for the documentary if you're still up for helping. Call me, okay?" she says, her goodbye as cold as the Vermont winter.

Mine is worse. I struggle to find the right words, to concoct some magical phrase that might shatter the fortress I've built around my heart. The disappointment in her beautiful eyes shatters me as I simply nod, my lips sealing off any word that might expose me.

Olivia climbs silently into the car, grips the steering wheel, takes a deep breath. Pulls onto the road, vanishes.

I stand frozen at the front door, my fingers numb from the cold, clutching the suitcases like some kind of fool.

And maybe I am, for watching the only person who's brought me back to happiness disappear without stopping her.

I blink back stupid tears that roll down my cheeks.

I've lost her forever.

Inside, the house feels like a barren wasteland, void of any signs of life. My girls are still with their father, and it's as if a deafening silence has claimed the atmosphere.

I let go. I slip back into the comfort of routine. You'll see me smiling in all my social media photos, but inside, I break a little more each day.

Olivia's words reverberate in my mind, an echo from a distant past: "Are you really going to settle for someone who doesn't hurt you?"

I don't aspire for more.

Yet, her memory haunts me. Each caress on my bare skin, the tender affection before sleep, our kisses, and the way she would hold me before drifting off. The mind-blowing orgasms she gifted me on our brief trip.

But then Emma's words return, heavy, flooding me with fear and doubt. They are a ghostly whisper reminding me that our fleeting love story is nothing more than a foolish fantasy.

I unpack the suitcase, and my eyes land on one of the T-shirts. Olivia wore it the last day we made love. We were naked on the bed, watching a silly Christmas movie, and she got cold. I handed her the first thing I found. It still smells like her.

I catch myself putting it separately in a drawer. I don't wash it with the rest of the clothes. Perhaps my subconscious wants to remember her scent. Or maybe it's just an excuse to torment myself with her absence.

Once my daughters return home, I force a smile. Soon, their Christmas anecdotes from their father's house run dry, and my smile fades. Even the clinking of the cutlery against the plate echoes too loud in the uncomfortable silence.

Angie finally speaks up, stepping into the adult role since her mother is acting like a complete jerk.

"Okay, Mom. Clearly, something's up. I don't remember you being this quiet even in the week after the divorce," she blurted out, raising her eyebrows as she spoke.

"I don't know what you mean," I respond, pretending to concentrate on cutting a piece of steak.

"You seem sad," Emma whispers.

"You always tell us there should be no secrets between us. You insist that we can tell you anything, whatever it is, and now you're the one hiding things. What a shitty example you're setting for your teenage daughters," Angie adds.

I stand up in anger. She was always a quiet child, but ever since she turned sixteen, she constantly challenges me.

"You can get mad all you want. Ground me or cut my allowance. But you know I'm right," she protests when I scold her.

"I told you nothing's wrong, and that's the end of this conversation," I snap, raising my voice louder than necessary.

"The woman you briefly mentioned on the phone… Is it Olivia Mitchell?" she inquires, and my heart stops.

"Why would you say that?"

"No need to be a genius. It's the easiest guess. You were best friends in high school, you go on a trip together, sharing a room, and dad gets all upset. It's like he was having a fit of jealousy every time someone mentioned her name," she explains, spreading her hands as if it's obvious to everyone but me.

I take a deep breath, wipe my sweaty hands on my jeans, and let the words flow. I describe our trip, let my eyes well up as emotions surge. I confess how incredibly happy I've been these days with her. I avoid mentioning that she gifted me with the best sex I can remember.

"Are you going to start dating?" Emma asks, her eyes filled with innocence.

"I think it's best for you two if I don't," I sigh.

Angie cuts me off, raising her voice while Emma looks on wide-eyed.

"The best thing for us is for you to be happy, damn it!" she yells.

"But…"

"Mom, we've talked about this, and we want you to be happy. You've been down since the divorce. Dad has moved on with his new girlfriend, it's time for you to do the same. We don't care if it's with a man, a woman, or just yourself.".

"OMG, don't say that to Mom," Emma whispers, a hint of caution in her voice.

"I didn't mean... I meant you can find happiness on your own. You don't need to...you know…" Angie begins, her words faltering, "I mean, if you do... that's okay, too. Most people do." Her gaze drops to her lap, a blush of embarrassment spreading across her cheeks.

A nervous giggle escapes me at the thought of my daughters picturing their mother in such a personal moment. The room fills with a contagious laughter, our hands clasped together, a trio of tomato-red faces.

"So, you knew all along?" I ask, attempting to regain my composure.

"We had our suspicions, even before you both left for Vermont. Olivia's not exactly subtle; her eyes practically shot hearts every time she looked at you. And then Dad started to refer to her as 'that lesbian woman', so we put two and two together. When you mentioned over the phone that there might be a woman... we figured it was her. By the way, we think she's super pretty," Angie adds, swiftly getting Emma's nod of approval.

"I think I've been an idiot," I confess, a sigh slipping from my lips.

"Did you tell her no?" Angie questions, her brow furrowed in concern.

"Worse. I ignored her all the way back. I was panicked."

"I wouldn't waste any more time. Text her," Angie advises.

"Text messages are for your generation. This deserves something much more personal," I confess, rising from the table to grab my coat and car keys.

My daughters exchange a knowing smile, but I barely notice. If only I could teleport myself to her doorstep, or better yet, find that time machine Olivia wished for as a Christmas gift and go back in time. Just two days would be enough.

"Mom, wait," Emma's voice echoes, halting me in my tracks. "Did you two kiss?"

Caught off guard, I close my eyes, a smile spreading across my lips. I bite down on my lower lip, causing Angie to burst out laughing, her hand covering her mouth to muffle the sound.

***

Olivia swings the door open, her eyes widening as they land on me, as if she's just seen a ghost. She's in a casual tee, with golden strands of hair escaping from a messy bun.

"This is for you. Twenty-five years late," I exhale, handing her a rose that's seen better days. "I'm sorry, there weren't any shops open on the way to your house, and this was all I could find at the gas station," I apologize, shrugging slightly.

Her beautiful green eyes, rarely vulnerable, glisten with unshed tears. They shine in the dim light, moist with emotion as she pulls me into a hug, her body trembling against the chill.

"This flower is the best Christmas gift I've ever received," she whispers into my ear, her voice a soft hiss.

"Before we go in, there's something else. Just a moment," I signal, asking her to wait as I clumsily attempt to hang a sprig of mistletoe on the doorframe.

The kiss that follows is nothing short of magical. There's an outpouring of emotions, feelings that flood us until we're both overwhelmed. Her hands cradle my cheeks, her forehead rests against mine, and I swear, the

"I love you" that follows sounds like the three most beautiful words I've ever heard.

***

The following day, at our New Year's Eve dinner, laughter and stories flow effortlessly around a dish of lamb that Olivia has masterfully prepared from a recipe she brought back from some distant land. The scent of rosemary and garlic fills the air, mingling with the warmth of our shared joy.

As the clock strikes midnight, we share a beautiful kiss, our daughters grinning and playfully raising their eyebrows in our direction.

"Here's to a New Year filled with joy," I declare, raising a glass of champagne.

"Of that, I have no doubt," Olivia responds, clinking her glass against mine.

We're smiling like two love-struck teenagers when my daughter Angie interrupts us.

"Emma and I are off to the school's New Year's Eve party. Behave yourselves, we're leaving you two alone," she teases, winking in a way that makes me blush.

Outside, fireworks explode in the sky, painting it with a riot of colors and marking the arrival of the New Year. Celebrations echo throughout the city, but as I take Olivia's hand and lead her to my bedroom, I know ours will have a special meaning. Now, it's clear that with Olivia, I'll become the woman I was always meant to be.

Epilog

Sam — One year later

The following Christmas, we return to the charming streets of Weston, Vermont, for the premiere of our documentary. We both wanted its first screening in this small town — a posthumous tribute to Sara Nelson and Mary Ellis. A testament to their struggles. Their tragic love story.

At the theater's entrance, a massive poster bearing their image stands tall, and judging by the full house, it seems the entire town has turned out.

But for us, this moment holds a special significance. This Christmas is a testament to my journey with Olivia last year. Twelve months together that have flown by in the blink of an eye.

Beth and John, Sara's and Mary's living relatives, sit next to us. Their presence is a touching bridge between the past and present.

Emma's eyes shine with excitement as she records everything on her phone to share with her friends. To my left, Angie is engaged in a lively conversation with Olivia.

If anyone had told me that raising two teenage daughters would be much easier with her by my side, I wouldn't have believed them. I was worried her wild spirit might be too much. Instead, not only have they welcomed Olivia into our family without the slightest hesitation, she's become their friend and confidante.

I still remember a few months ago when Angie experienced her first heartbreak. She sought out Olivia, not me, her mother. Rather than feeling jealous, I thought it was endearing.

"Guys are becoming more and more confusing, Liv," I remember her saying, resting her head on Olivia's shoulder in the same way I did at her age. *"One day, he's flooding me with sweet messages; the next, he's ignoring me."*

"Sorry to break it to you, but things don't get much better with age," Olivia jokes. *"Still, you're very mature for your age. Don't waste your time trying to get someone's attention who doesn't deserve you."*

Emma squeezes my hand as the lights dim and our documentary flickers to life. As it unfolds, every sigh from the audience buoys my pride like a peacock's display.

The documentary captures moments of joy and discovery but also of heartache. I can't stop the tears coursing down my cheeks when the story of how Mary learned of Sara's death is narrated. I think at least half the audience is crying or trying not to.

Olivia has perfectly captured the raw suffering of that loss through Mary's diary entries. Luckily, she's also managed to convey a powerful and beautiful message, a heartfelt tribute to the legacy of these two brave women who fought for forbidden love in a time long past.

As the final credits roll and the audience rises to applaud, a deep sense of peace and satisfaction washes over me. Sara and Mary have been an inspiration, helping me embrace love rather than being trapped by fear and doubt.

Later, my daughters gave me the courage to open my heart, to seek happiness with Olivia. They are my world, and I can never thank them enough for giving me that final push.

"This place is so beautiful. It's impossible not to fall in love here," Emma exclaims, linking her arm with mine as we stroll through the snow-laden streets.

"It's impossible not to fall in love with someone like your mother," Olivia corrects, causing both Emma and me to blush furiously.

She kisses me then, as tiny snowflakes begin to fall around us.

"Ahem, Liv, better save that for the hotel room. Your daughters are here, and we're all freezing," Angie teases.

It's the first time she's implied Olivia's motherly role in a comment. Emma does it, but I suppose at thirteen, it's been easier for her to accept.

Hand in hand, we walk through the snowy streets towards the hotel. This small town nurtured the first, fragile buds of our love. I've returned transformed, stronger, bound to Olivia in a bond that nothing and no one can break.

With her, every day is an adventure. Every minute worth living. She makes me feel special, loved. Desired and protected. Fulfilled.

Today, I am the woman I always wanted to be.

Other Books by the Same Author

If you liked this book, you'll probably like the following books as well:

Trilogy Watson Memorial Hospital
Interconnected stand-alone books

Doctor Stone: A Sapphic Medical Romance

A decade ago, a tragic surgery forever altered the lives of Dr. Jackie Stone and Sarah Taylor. Haunted by the loss of that patient, Dr. Stone has since immersed herself in her work, believing that if she stays busy, she can escape the pain of her past.

Sarah Taylor, now a determined intern at Manhattan's prestigious Watson Memorial Hospital, finds herself under the supervision of the very doctor who was present during her brother's ill-fated surgery ten years ago.

As she strives to become a renowned surgeon, Sarah must grapple with the emotional weight of working in the same hospital where her brother died, under the watchful eye of the woman who couldn't save him.

Don't miss this riveting sapphic medical romance exploring the intricate dance of forgiveness, healing, and the transformative power of love.

Doctor Torres: A Sapphic Medical Romance

At 27, Nicole Hunt is a rising star in health and wellness, captivating audiences with her dynamic podcast and entertaining TikTok presence. In a special series for Heart Month, she sets her sights on interviewing some of the nation's most prominent medical professionals, including the reclusive Dr. Inés Torres.

Dr. Torres is a 40-year-old distinguished cardiologist with a reputation as steely as the scalpel she wields. Her life revolves entirely around her work, leaving no room for love or leisure.

As the effervescent Nicole steps into Dr. Torres's strictly regimented world, sparks fly, and an unexpected connection forms between the two women. Can Nicole's warmth and charisma melt Dr. Torres's icy exterior and unlock the door to a new, fulfilling chapter in her life?

Immerse yourself in this captivating sapphic medical romance, a heartwarming journey of love, healing, and the power of letting go.

Doctor Harris: A Sapphic Medical Romance

A doctor in love with a resident.

A resident in love with a patient.

A patient in love with herself.

Dr. Rachel Harris has always played by the book, until a mysterious woman arrives at the hospital after a grave accident, sending her world into a tailspin.

As the patient lies in an induced coma, Dr. Harris finds solace in her daydreams, crafting an enchanting romance with this enigmatic woman. Her fantasies provide an escape from her otherwise regimented life, stirring feelings she's never experienced before.

However, reality comes crashing down when the patient finally awakens, revealing herself to be a moody, self-absorbed woman who bears no resemblance to the person Rachel had come to love in her mind. As Dr. Harris grapples with her unexpected feelings, she must confront the blurred lines between fantasy and reality, desire and responsibility.

Don't miss this mesmerizing sapphic medical romance that delves into the complexities of love, self-discovery, and the journey of personal growth.

Crossed Destinies: A Sapphic Billionaire Romance

The CEO of a technology company whose methods border the limits of ethics.

A journalist in search of the truth and eager to prove herself.

What can go wrong?

From their first encounter, an undeniable chemistry draws them together. Yet, their professional ambitions threaten to drive a wedge between them.

As Sarah digs deeper into the inner workings of Hailey's empire, she uncovers shocking secrets that threaten to expose the dark underbelly behind its success. Torn between protecting the woman she's falling for and revealing the truth, Sarah grapples with the biggest decision of her life.

Will she prioritize her commitment to journalistic integrity and unveil the truth, or will her deepening feelings for Hailey cloud her judgment?

Can her relationship survive the pressure, or will it blow up?

Passions flare, and ethical lines blur in this tension-filled romance set in the high-stakes world of corporate finance. When matters of the heart collide with the quest for truth, the fallout could destroy careers, relationships, and even lives.

Tie Break: A Sapphic Sports Romance

Brooke McKlain is a household name for tennis fans.

Elena has no idea who she is. She just knows she's ruining her life.

When Brooke decides to take a much-needed break at a luxury hotel in Hawaii, she doesn't expect that the woman who challenged her from the very first moment will show her what love is.

Elena will make her question many things, and now love spins onto her court, revealing what she's been missing.

But their worlds are too different, and things are never as easy as they seem... especially when the public image you want to give outweighs your feelings.

A Cup of Love. A Second Chance Sapphic Romance.

Phoenix is about to realize the dream of a lifetime. Her small café in the heart of Edinburgh is ready to open. It's been years in the making, but it's been worth it. The opening is booming, and the café fills up with friends and family.

But when Erin Miller shows up by surprise, it can only

mean one thing: trouble.

Why is she back in Edinburgh?

Phoenix doesn't quite remember how she came to be friends with someone like Erin Miller, the high school rebel girl, the same one who broke hearts without thinking about the consequences.

One crazy night, some alcohol and something happened that Phoenix would rather forget forever.

The next day, Erin disappeared...for six long years.

What was she doing now at the opening of her café?

Why did he still feel the same butterflies every time Erin Miller smiled?

She says she's changed.

Is that possible, and can someone like Erin Miller change?

Does she deserve a second chance, or will she disappear again as she did six years ago?

Nashville. A Lesbian Romance

Sex, drugs, and rock and roll.

Jackie Thomas' life could be summed up in that mythical sentence.

After leaving home at the age of 16, she wandered around the country, making a living in various bands as a singer or guitarist.

Now, at 28, she has risen to the top as the lead singer of the Black Magic, a heavy metal band with a legion of loyal fans.

Mary Crawford is a rising figure in country music. Dubbed by the press as the "Princess of Nashville," she is making her way in a band with her two older sisters under the strict guidance of her father. He conditions every aspect of her musical career and her life.

Sparks fly between them when they must travel to Las Vegas as judges for a talent show. The rock star's strong and irresponsible personality clashes with the good judgment of the country singer. Still, they soon discover that they have more in common than they first thought. After all, Las Vegas is a city full of magic.

But does what happens in Vegas always stay in Vegas?

YOUNG ADULT SAPPHIC ROMANCE

Liar: A Young Adult "fake date" LGBTQ+ Romance

Nina Álvarez is living the dream.

She's the high school basketball team captain, a social media sensation, and one of the most popular girls at school. But when a misplaced comment goes viral, Nina's future comes crashing down.

With accusations of homophobia threatening to destroy everything she's worked for, Nina devises a daring plan: fake-date Alexia Taylor, a proud and openly gay girl from her high school.

Alexia is her polar opposite. She's a brilliant, introverted aspiring scientist with her sights set on NASA. And she wants nothing to do with Nina's scheme.

However, when Alexia's best friend Cris gets involved, she soon finds herself unable to say no.

As Nina and Alexia play their roles in this high-stakes game of pretend, they find themselves drawn to each other in ways they never expected. Amidst the whirl-wind of high school drama, basketball games, and social media scandals, the two girls discover that sometimes, the line between love and lies isn't so clear.

Operation Vanessa

Riley, the high school resident rebel, never thought she'd fall for anyone—especially not Vanessa, the untouchable cheerleading squad captain.

In a world where social expectations and invisible barriers dictate the rules, they are on opposite sides of the high school spectrum.

But love won't be ignored. Overwhelmed by her feelings, Riley turns to Alexia, a straight-A student with a gift for words. Together, they hatch a daring plan inspired by Cyrano de Bergerac to capture the cheerleader's heart.

Milton Keynes UK
Ingram Content Group UK Ltd.
UKHW010928231123
433129UK00001B/194